OCT 04 2022

The WHISPERING FOG

The WHISPERING FOG

Landra Jennings

CLARION BOOKS

AN IMPRINT OF HARPERCOLLINS*PUBLISHERS*

Clarion Books is an imprint of HarperCollins Publishers.

The Whispering Fog

ISBN 978-0-35-867455-9

Typography by Marcie Lawrence
22 23 24 25 26   PC/LSCC   10 9 8 7 6 5 4 3 2 1

First Edition

For Mom

Chapter One

NEVE AND ROSE were always together.

Two pieces to a puzzle. Two blades of a scissor. Two branches of the same tree.

They were named after the devoted sisters in "Snow-White and Rose-Red" by the Brothers Grimm. Rose had auburn hair and rosy cheeks. And Neve, born eleven months later, had hair so blond it was nearly white. The pronunciation "Nehv" was hard for people to remember, but the name Neve meant "snow."

And they had turned out to be as close as the sisters in the fairy tale.

"There's plenty of room in here," Neve said to Rose one October morning.

In the cardboard box, she meant. Where she was currently sitting.

She'd been making the boxes for years. They started out as discards from places like Publix and Furniture Barn and ended up as all sorts of things—houses, ships, machines. Some more elaborate than others. *Neve's art*, Rose called them.

That particular day, it was a big packing box from their recent move. Neve had made a door and a window, shingled a roof with construction paper, and created a chimney from a paper-towel tube; it doubled as a periscope. The walls were a collage of images from magazines: misty forests, roaming bears, shining birds. She called it Magic House and kept it in their bedroom. The inside smelled of a lavender sachet and the orange slices she was having for breakfast.

"I've got a pillow for you too," she said out the little window. "You can finish your chapter for language arts. It's definitely not too crowded." The box *was* extra-large, the best size. She also had a book light and Rose's favorite blanket, but Rose already knew that.

"Maybe in a minute," Rose said from the closet. "I'm working on our clothes."

Neve bit into an orange slice. They'd been in the same grade since kindergarten (Neve having turned five two days before the cutoff), and in seventh grade, she knew, clothes were important. Even more so because three weeks earlier, they'd moved to Etters, South Carolina, after the school year had already begun, and kids were still deciding what they thought of them. Neve just didn't know (or care) what looked good, so, as usual, she left it to Rose. Neve was in charge of the homework. "Well, what about the math? You said you wanted to look it over."

Rose emerged from the closet, arms full of clothes. "That's right, I do. But can we do it on the bus? Come on out. I've got an idea that's going to be a-*maz*-ing."

"Okay." Neve closed the paper curtain and it was dark again.

She wasn't in a hurry to get out. She felt calmer inside her boxes —safe, really. Rose liked the calm too, she said, it was just that she got restless, needed to move around after a few minutes. When Mom and Dad fought, Neve and Rose had often gone into one of Neve's boxes. They'd curl up back to back, or sometimes Rose's hand would find Neve's. The two of them against the world. A team.

In the new house, it was different. Rose had turned thirteen right before they moved. She'd grown, she said. She didn't really fit into a box. And she wasn't happy with the move, the house, the fact that she didn't have a cell phone. She wasn't happy with *Mom*. Rose and Mom's arguments had replaced Mom and Dad's.

Separated. It's complicated.

That was Mom's explanation for why they were moving out of the old house. Neve didn't think it was as complicated as all that. The reason for her parents' separation seemed pretty clear. She kept it hidden in her chest, the reason. Unfortunately, it refused to lie still in there. It scrabbled around, paining her wherever she went. And the more she tried to not-think about it, the more it demanded to be thought about. She rubbed her chest in the spot.

"You are going to *love* this." Rose's muffled voice came through the paper-towel tube. She probably meant a new hairstyle or some new makeup.

Neve appreciated that Rose made them look good, she did, it was just that she missed silly-hair days and matching-shirt days. And making commercials for their YouTube channel for products they liked (Rose did the acting, Neve the sets). But between shopping, friends, school plays, and tennis, Rose didn't have much extra time anymore. In fact, she always seemed to be in a hurry to get to the next thing on the schedule.

"Fifteen minutes, Neve."

Neve climbed out and Rose immediately pounced, enveloping Neve in the scent of apple and honey shampoo as she flat-ironed Neve's hair. They both had long hair because of the styles Rose liked to try. Rose had Neve's clothes laid out on the bed. An outfit Neve didn't recognize—green skirt and a gray T-shirt with a pink flower on the front.

"What do you think?" Rose said about the outfit.

"So cute." Neve might actually have preferred jeans, but Rose had taken charge of their clothes since that time in fourth grade when Neve wore a much-loved (although admittedly ugly and way too big) plaid shirt to school and was made fun of by practically everybody. These days, they always looked *just right,* according to Rose, who loved H&M and Target but was also a genius Goodwill shopper.

"I packed our tennis bags," Rose said. "Got that blue tank you like." Their old courts and coach were a forty-minute drive away, but they were still going there after school to practice while their parents *figured everything out.* They both played competitive tennis and didn't want to get behind.

"Thanks," Neve said. "What about granola bars? Our water bottles?"

"Got them." Rose smelled of mint toothpaste. Her face was close while she did something to Neve's eyebrows with a little brush. Rose had covered the freckles on her nose with makeup, Neve noticed.

"Sunscreen and visors?" The sun was friend to neither of them, even in October.

"Good call. Let's grab some before we go." Rose moved away to dig in her jewelry box.

Neve's eyes met Mom's in the mirror. Mom was in the hall, wearing sweats, her gray-blond hair in a topknot. Though she carried a broom, she'd obviously been watching them, not sweeping, as she wore a faint frown. She wasn't very strict about them wearing makeup but often said Neve was pretty without it and, what's more, was perfectly capable of choosing her own clothes. In fact, Mom had been talking a lot lately about Neve becoming more independent. *You've got a lot of talents and ideas all your own, Neve. You don't have to do everything Rose thinks you should do. And you and Rose don't have to do everything together.*

Before Mom could say anything along those lines, Neve jumped up. "It's nearly time for the bus. We don't want to be late."

"Look at li'l sis. So *on it* today. Give it here," Rose said.

They did their secret handshake—a complicated sequence of hand movements, claps, and snaps—while Neve avoided looking at Mom.

Every day of Neve's life, it'd been Neve and Rose, Rose and Neve. Neve hadn't spoken a word until she was three years old because Rose had talked for her. Rose knew what Neve wanted before Neve knew it herself. And Neve calmed Rose down when she got worked up (which was often) and watched her back. Rose wouldn't be able to get by without Neve; Neve was sure of that. Neve planned on them going to the same college and living next door to each other when they were old. Maybe even marrying brothers, that sort of thing.

Neve and Rose did not leave each other. They did not.

Chapter Two

THEIR NEW SCHOOL seemed fine. Except for what was in the woods.

Neve and Rose were in the cafeteria at lunch, at a table with some other kids, sitting side by side, as usual.

Rose was talking. And that was the usual state of things too. She speculated with a few girls about who'd go out for the tennis team next year, and every now and then she joked around with this guy named Sammy and some other guys from the basketball team who were sitting at the next table. Rose always made friends fast. On the tennis team, at summer camp, in drama club. It was easy for her, all the talking.

Neve was not talking. As was *her* usual, she was tuning a lot of the chatter out. She rubbed at the ache in her chest while she inspected the questionable items on her lunch tray. Despite being hungry, she'd gotten no further than picking up her fork. The cafeteria smelled musty. The cold of the chair seeped through her flimsy skirt. And the kids' voices echoed in the cavernous room. Though there were several hundred students at Etters Middle, the building could have held a lot more kids, and the din was more subdued than at their old school.

There was something else Neve didn't quite like but she couldn't put her finger on it. It might have been the school itself, the old brick structure with its watchful air and winding halls. Or it might have been the sky outside, overcast as it had been for days now, gray and purple clouds warning of rain. Or it might have been the fact that students here walked with their heads down, whistling or humming as they hurried between classes.

At least Rose hadn't noticed the something. She hadn't said anything and Neve hadn't mentioned it. She didn't want Rose to worry and get a migraine. Especially since it was just a feeling.

Rose interrupted Neve's thoughts. "What do you think, Neve?"

Neve hadn't followed the conversation and didn't know what Rose was asking about. "Yep," she said. "Totally agree."

Rose beamed and started talking again. But . . . her foot jiggled like it did when she was nervous, and she hadn't touched her pasta. So maybe Rose *had* noticed something. Neve would ask when they were alone.

The school being a little off was not a *real* issue anyway. It was probably Neve's imagination. The move had just been so upsetting, it was coloring everything else. The secret in her chest pinched.

"Did you know that tomato juice is the official beverage of Ohio?"

Neve gave a little jump. She hadn't noticed the girl to her left. Short strawberry curls and wire-rimmed glasses. Neve thought her name was Piper. Piper was very into tomatoes and had made an interesting point in science class about the scientific name for a tomato, which meant "wolf peach."

"I didn't know states had official beverages," Neve said. "What's South Carolina's?"

Piper nodded at Neve's tray. "Milk. I can't drink it, though. I'm allergic."

"I'm allergic to wheat," Neve offered. She poked at the beef. It had some sort of breading on it, so she probably shouldn't have taken it.

A pause. "Um, so . . . I heard you live off State Highway Twenty-Eight, out past the water tower and the old Shell station?"

Neve looked up. Piper's face was red, like her favorite vegetable. She seemed to be holding her breath.

"You *heard* that?" Neve said. "Why would anyone be talking about where we live?" Their house was at the edge of a large wood and they had no neighbors as far as Neve could tell.

"Etters is a small town. We haven't had anyone move here in a while. Mostly, everyone moves away. And to tell the truth, I heard my pops mentioning it to my aunt. We used to live close by there. Are you in that house by the lake?" Piper ever so casually opened a bag of carrot sticks.

"The house we're renting is by a lake. I don't know if it's the one you're talking about."

"See, I wanted to talk to you about something. But not here—"

"Neve, did you forget?" Rose was standing, brows lifted.

Her tray was in her hand.

"Oh, right. Math," Neve said. She dropped her fork. They had worked on Rose's homework on the bus ride, but she wanted to review it.

"Don't abandon me now," Rose said to Neve. And to the others: "Later, guys. We're going to the classroom early. *Emergency* study session."

The girls made unhappy sounds, though several of them would see Rose again next period. Neve felt a secret satisfaction. *She* was the one Rose always needed in the end. And Neve was the only one who knew Rose actually worried about things. Like math, for instance. It wasn't just for show.

Neve stood with her tray. "See you," she said to Piper.

"See you when I see you," Piper said.

"Like in science class, right?"

"Yes, that's when I'll see you." Piper waved a carrot stick.

The table of kids seemed to deflate when Rose left. Neve was used to that.

"I'm stressing," Rose said when they got to the hall.

"You did a lot of talking and you didn't eat anything. You're not getting a migraine, are you?"

"No, it's not that. Lunch was fun. Let's sit down and I'll tell you."

The math classroom was empty and smelled of dry-erase markers and old textbooks. The walls were covered in Halloween-themed student art. A witch made up of different geometric shapes glued together hung over their heads.

"So," Rose said. "Jody just got me by the drink machine and told me not to worry but that the kids tell scary stories about the woods where we live. Like, people think it's cursed. I thought something seemed wrong for it to be so deserted around our house. She says she didn't tell me earlier because it's just stories and she didn't want to freak me out. But I *am* freaked out."

"What kind of stories?"

"That something dangerous lives in the woods. That if kids walk in, they'll be swallowed up and they'll never come out again. Can you believe it?"

"Huh." That girl Piper had wanted to talk about where they lived too.

"Do you think it could be true? Like, really?"

Rose had been upset enough about *why* they'd had to move; she didn't need to be upset about *where* they'd ended up. "No, I don't," Neve said, rubbing at the pain in her chest. "Kids just like telling scary stories. Remember how Catherine Finatti kept putting fake blood around camp to scare everybody?"

"This was different. Jody wasn't faking anything. She seemed really worried for us."

"Yeah. The kids around here need more to do." Neve pulled out her notebook. "The test is Friday. Don't you want to review?"

"Yes, I do," Rose said, studying Neve's face—to see if she was worried, Neve knew. "That lipstick is good on you. I knew it would be," Rose added, the comment probably a cover for her looking.

Neve took out her colored gel pens. She kept her face carefully blank. Those strange stories on top of her weird feeling about the school, well, that *did* make her a little worried. But there was no need to upset Rose over nothing. Neve would talk to Piper first. If there was truly anything to worry about, then Neve would tell Rose and together they could make a plan. "You can use the purple pen. That's an A-plus color for sure." Neve turned the corners of her lips up for good measure as she held out the box.

"My hero. You've saved me yet again." Rose was back to beaming.

* * *

Neve wasn't happy about taking a class without Rose. She'd never done that before. But somebody had assigned Neve to honors science without asking her what she wanted. Normally, she dragged her feet getting there, but that day she hurried into class looking for Piper.

Neve spotted her right away. Those strawberry curls, that yellow tie-dyed shirt. But the teacher had already rearranged the desks so the students were in their groups for the mutualism project. Piper wasn't in Neve's group, so Neve would have to wait until after class.

She walked over to her own group: Sammy, he of the long, shiny black hair that Rose said was gorgeous; Aniyah, who had box braids, a nose ring, and a cross-body purse Neve admired; and Toni, a girl with spiky hair who rubbed her face a lot and often put her head down on the desk midconversation.

"Did you finish your index cards?" Aniyah said, getting right down to business.

Neve nodded and rummaged in her backpack. Each group member had chosen a pair of organisms that worked together for mutual gain. They'd drawn them on cards and would work on animating them in a video on their group's assigned Chromebook. Neve had chosen bees and flowers.

"Those look awesome!" Sammy said about Neve's cards, so loudly that Neve flinched. Sammy was super-popular and super-energetic. He always talked louder and smiled bigger than she expected. And ever since Mrs. Michaels had hung Neve's cell diagram on the Excellence board the week Neve arrived, everyone was acting like she was this great artist. It was a little more attention than she wanted.

"Thanks," Neve said, smiling but careful not to show her braces. Rose hadn't needed braces herself, but she always said smiling without teeth was best when you had braces.

They spread out their cards. Aniyah had taken oxpeckers and rhinos. Toni had chosen sea anemones and clown fish. And Sammy had picked humans and intestinal bacteria.

"*Why* did I pick intestinal bacteria?" Sammy said. "Nobody should have to picture that."

"Should we add a note about parasitism?" Aniyah poked at her cards. "Because oxpeckers can pick at rhinos so much, they get infected wounds. It's *not* good."

"Or what about organisms that benefit multiple creatures?" Toni said. "Should that be a separate section?"

Neve thought they should have two sections at most, one with examples of where mutualism worked and another showing where it didn't quite.

If Rose were there, Neve would say that to Rose and then Rose would make sure the group did it.

But Rose was not there, so Neve said nothing. Instead, she took out her colored pens and put the finishing touches on a flower.

"Maybe Neve can help me with my cards," Sammy said, eyeing hers. "Sprinkle them with her magic dust. Keep them from looking so bad. What do you say, Neve?"

Neve glanced over. Sammy had done his drawings in black pen. They were good; they could just use some color. Neve nodded.

"So . . . you *do* think they're bad?" Sammy said, his big smile disappearing for once.

"No. They're really good."

Big smile again. "Thanks. You going to join the art club? We're working on faces next month."

Neve felt briefly surprised that Sammy was in art club. She'd already put him in the category of basketball players. "I don't think so," she said. Faces, particularly eyes, *were* something Neve would love to work on. But Rose had said no to art club.

Aniyah and Sammy launched into a discussion about how

to organize the presentation. Toni didn't join in because she was too busy snoring softly, head on the desk. Neve added color to Sammy's drawings.

By the time class was over, Sammy and Aniyah hadn't agreed on much of anything except that Sammy's cards now looked awesome.

When the bell rang, Neve grabbed her backpack and hurried to catch Piper before she left the classroom. "I wanted to talk about what you said at lunch."

Piper made her eyes big, inclining her head toward her group; the kids were packing up. "You mean about tomatoes?" she said loudly. "How there are more colors than merely red? Yellow, pink, white, purple—"

"No," Neve said. "About where we live."

Piper put a finger to her lips and the two of them went into the hall. As they walked, Piper ate a tomato like an apple. "I probably shouldn't have said anything. But I heard my pops mention you'd moved out there, and I thought . . ."

"Thought what?"

Piper swallowed. "I thought you should know some *facts*. People have disappeared from around where you live. I wanted to warn you."

"People? What people? Are you sure?"

Piper blinked several times. "Keep a close watch on your sister is all I've got to say. A *really* close watch. And your sister should keep a close watch on *you*. I've got to go."

Neve caught Piper's arm, nearly causing her to drop her tomato. "Wait, you can't leave me with that. Who disappeared? When?"

Piper's face crumpled. "My sister. Two years ago."

"That's horrible . . . I'm so sorry. She just vanished?" The warning bell rang. Neve was probably going to be late for keyboarding class. She patted Piper on the back.

"They said she ran away, but she didn't. And she's not the only one. There've been more girls. And people just *forget*. They move on. It's *not* okay."

Rose was down the hall in a doorway, frantically waving for Neve to come to class.

"Thank you for telling me." Neve felt bad leaving Piper while she was upset. "Can I have your phone number? We can talk more later." That might actually prove hard to do. Neve and Rose didn't have cell phones, so Neve would have to wrestle Mom's phone away from both her *and* Rose.

Piper's hand shook as she wrote her number on Neve's notebook. "No matter what you hear, my sister did not run away. That is just not what happened. She was *taken*."

Chapter Three

THEIR BUS STOP was the last one. The other kids were long gone.

As the nearly empty school bus rattled along the country road, Neve looked out over the open fields and abandoned houses and thought about what Piper had said. It *was* pretty remote here. There was the old Shell gas station, the pumps removed. The water tower, eaten up by rust and kudzu; someone had spray-painted *Reed loves Bianca* on it and then crossed it out with a big red *X*. And the white church with a picket fence around it. Clearly no one went to services there. Plywood covered the windows, and weeds had spread through the walkways and the small graveyard.

But just because a place was remote didn't mean it was dangerous. And it had been two years since Piper's sister disappeared. *Two years.* That was a really long time.

Rose leaned across Neve toward the window. "Jody was right about this place," Rose said. "It does look cursed. What's the word? *Blighted.* Even that mailbox. Look at that thing."

Vines smothered the mailbox; it hung open like it was gasping for air. "Looks more like it was attacked by a crowbar.

Besides, places can't really be cursed."

"It's so run-down and deserted. I don't get what Mom was thinking."

Neve knew what Mom had been thinking. She'd seen the old-fashioned-looking ad: *Expansive acreage! Room for all your creative endeavors! Priceless outdoor time for your youngsters!* Not to mention the rent was dirt cheap.

At first, Neve had shared Mom's view: The birds and animals. The lake. The piney woods. It all seemed magical. She'd taken a deep breath there and felt at home in a way she never had back in Acadia Lakes, with its cookie-cutter houses, tiny backyards, orderly streets. It was as if they'd stepped through a portal into another world, not simply driven forty minutes east.

After listening to Rose's complaints for weeks, though, and now the kids' warnings . . . Neve wasn't sure what to think. But, as she often did when Rose got worried, Neve went hard in the other direction. "It's what the country looks like. You're just not used to it."

Rose appeared doubtful.

The bus came to a stop at their gravel drive and they walked up to the front. "See ya, Mrs. Peterson. Stay stylish," Rose said.

"I've got a doozy for you tomorrow." Another wacky hat, Mrs. Peterson meant. The elderly bus driver had a fondness for hats, the wackier, the better. That afternoon's was a cowboy hat with a skull and crossbones.

"Can't wait to see it." Rose and the driver high-threed. It'd been only a few weeks but they already had a signature hello and goodbye, like a high five but with fingers. Mrs. Peterson was missing a couple.

The driver swung the door open and Neve followed Rose off the bus. "Stay safe," Mrs. Peterson said.

The driver said *Stay safe* each and every day. Surely she didn't mean anything special by it? It wasn't as if they were going anywhere *un*safe.

Goose bumps rose on Neve's arms. It wasn't particularly cold for October, but it didn't take much for her to get goose bumps. She was thin. Too thin, or so she'd been told. Unlike Rose, who had a more athletic build.

Neve glanced back at the bus doors. Mrs. Peterson was watching her through the glass. The driver touched her hat to Neve and left in a roar of dust and fumes.

Neve let out a breath. It was a strange sort of day.

"Guess we'll see whatever weird cleaning project Mom's doing now," Rose said.

Mom had been cleaning since they got there, talking about *clean* and *happy* as if the two words were the same. It *was* a little much, but Neve didn't respond because she didn't want to get Rose started about Mom.

As they fell silent, Neve could hear the aliveness around them. Things rustling in the grass, buzzing in the air, whispering in the trees. She'd never lived anyplace where that stuff was all she could hear. There was no traffic. No lawn mowers. No Mr. Brewer with his loud parties and ever-present weed-eater.

They really were in an isolated place. But the sun peeked through the clouds, and birds chirped happily, as if they welcomed the girls. As if they welcomed *her*. Over the past few weeks, she'd explored all around the overgrown backyard and the lake. She'd seen nothing frightening except a single copperhead. It felt like a place from a fairy tale.

They kicked up gravel as they walked. Neve glanced down at Rose's blue Converse sneakers. Dad had bought those, she knew, for Rose's birthday. Maybe Mom could get Neve some just like them and then they could match. Or maybe matching shoes weren't okay in seventh grade. She wasn't sure.

"I told Mr. Simmons we'd do the drama club," Rose said. "It's Thursdays after school. We'll need to get Mom to pick us up."

Neve had enjoyed helping with costumes and masks when Rose played Nala in *The Lion King Jr.* at their old school last year. "Sounds fun."

"And by the way, the costumes don't get made by drama club. They get made by art club," Rose said, as if she knew what Neve was thinking. "That's on Thursdays too." She didn't say anything else.

Why was Rose mentioning art club again? She'd already said she didn't want to do it. The comment was somehow irritating to Neve, like discovering a pebble in her shoe. "Yes, but I might want to try out for a speaking part this year." That wasn't true. Neve had no intention of trying out for a speaking part. But she'd find something she could do in drama club. Maybe she could help Rose with her lines.

She could feel Rose looking at her like she might add something else, but Neve said, "Let's go ask Mom about Thursdays." And she jogged around to the back of the house.

Mom had left a bunch of tools — rakes and shovels — sitting out on the planting beds, but her car was gone. A sack of fertilizer was abandoned on the driveway.

"She really does not know what she's doing," Rose said, coming up behind Neve.

Mom was going to grow plants and sell them, or so she'd said. Not that she'd ever done that before. Mom was usually busy year-round with a container-potting business. She'd fill porches with flowers in the warm seasons and with decorations in the cold. She ought to be doing planters of Halloween stuff this time of year: scowling witches and bats, grinning skulls. Neve and Rose agreed on this point: out here was a pretty impractical place to set up shop.

They found a note from Mom in the kitchen. She'd gone to a meeting. They were supposed to have the snacks she'd left for them, and Dad would be coming to take them to practice.

No phone, then, to call Piper. No e-mails either. Mom was apparently in no hurry to get the internet and Wi-Fi set up.

"I'll bet she's meeting with that attorney," Rose said. "I hate that attorney."

"What's wrong with him?"

"I don't know. He's just got that fake smile. And why does

Mom have to get an attorney anyway? I wish none of this had happened."

Neve didn't answer that. She just rubbed at the pain in her chest. In the refrigerator were Halloween snacks: Bread sticks cut to look like bones. Brownies with red gel dripped on them to look like blood. "Hey, Mom made cheddar witch fingers. Aren't those your favorite?" Neve said. Rose had left the kitchen, though.

She was in the family room, right next to the tiny kitchen. The house was small, cramped, and crowded, according to Rose. Neve thought it was cozy.

"I am so *over* themed food—ouch!" Rose said. "Mom's moved furniture again."

Rose was rubbing her knee. The furniture was indeed in different spots. The painting—a new one that looked like someone had thrown paint at the canvas—had been moved too and was now over the weird-looking divan, also new. Neve shrugged. "She's used to Dad setting up that stuff, I guess."

Dad was particular. He wanted this kind of paint color, that type of couch, this sort of television. Maybe Mom didn't know how to want something for herself, so she kept rearranging.

"I am so sick of this." Rose headed back to the door. "I'm going to do some drills. Want to come?"

"Yup." Neve walked to the bedroom to change out of the green skirt. She didn't love the tennis drills so much, but they helped, she knew that. She and Rose were USTA tournament players, and wins factored into their state rankings. Back when she was nine, Neve had gotten as high as twentieth in the state. Now that she was older—well, she tried not to check the rankings too much anymore.

∗ ∗ ∗

Neve meant to do the drills. She really did.

But when she walked into the bedroom, she noticed a slim book on the desk. She ran a finger across the faded red cover. The book was old, the gilt and title worn away. Mom must've found it somewhere and left it for her. It wasn't for Rose; she wasn't so much into reading. No, the book was for Neve.

Intrigued, Neve took the book and climbed into Magic House box. She would read for only a minute. Or maybe two.

The inside of the box smelled of the lavender sachet and was gloriously quiet. The box was just big enough for her to sit up in, but she leaned back on her pillow, snuggled inside a fleece blanket, and clicked on a book light. She was safe here from anyone looking over her shoulder, anyone telling her she shouldn't be reading "weird" books, as Dad called her fantasy novels. And she suspected this one would fall into that category. She opened the book, carefully. The spine was cracked and some of the pages were loose.

A musty smell came from the book, as if it hadn't been opened in a while. It had pictures, and dark illustrations of vines appeared to weave through the pages. The words were in an old-fashioned, curly script. No title page or publication information, though it looked like a fairy tale. She turned to the beginning of the book and started to read.

Once upon a time there was a young woman who could not find anyone to love her in a way that satisfied her. No one's devotion was worthy of her beauty and charms. Tiring of the world, she took a great ship to a desolate land and went to live alone in a boggy wood. There, she bore triplet daughters. Finally, the young mother thought. Someone to love her as she deserved.

To raise them, the young mother used her skills in the magical arts as well as a knife and a spell book given to her by her own mother. The young mother's potions soothed the babes; her swamp creatures—the foxes, birds, and snakes —guarded them; and her songs enthralled them.

But as the babes grew and began to walk and talk and get into mischief, the young mother's difficulties increased. Having three small daughters meant laboring from dawn to dusk and then some, magic or no. One day while fetching water, the young mother glanced at her reflection and found that she was no longer fair. That would not do, she thought. That would not do at all.

She left her daughters in the care of an old goat named Mildred and traveled to the land of the dwarves, renowned for their wisdom. The dwarves offered the young mother a golden cup. If she drank the elixir that appeared in the cup each day at dawn, the bloom on her cheeks would linger. The cup, however, came at a price. As she possessed nothing else of value she could part with, the young mother was forced to trade one of her daughters. The dwarves came and took the daughter away.

The two remaining daughters grew and grew and became young women themselves, but their mother did not appear to age a single day. The girls spied on their mother and discovered the morning ritual with the golden cup. Their suspicions were confirmed one morning when a dwarf appeared while their mother was out. The sister was defective, the dwarf claimed. She had died in less than a decade. The bargain was void. The daughters knew their sister had gone to live with the dwarves, though they'd never understood why. They were horrified to learn of the bargain. They claimed to know nothing of the golden cup. The dwarf went away unsatisfied.

As the months and years flew by, the daughters' resentment increased tenfold. Their mother was, they determined, actually aging, albeit at a slow pace. What would happen when the mother noticed this? Would she sacrifice another daughter for more magic to extend her beauty and her life? That would not do, they thought. That would not do at all. For they loved each other dearly.

And so, one night when the mother was sleeping, the daughters stabbed her with the knife until she was dead. They took the book and the golden cup and resolved to share equally in the magic of both. Wielding the book, they became *more and more powerful. They increased the protections and enchantments on their home to shield themselves from the dwarves, entrenched themselves more firmly in the swamp, and drew more and more creatures to them to feed their spells and themselves.*

This arrangement worked perfectly for many long years. But then the beauty of the girls faded, age began to wear upon them, and it became clear that the elixir of one cup was not enough for two.

The door of the bedroom creaked and Rose galloped in. Her voice was right next to the box when she said, "Are you in there? What are you doing? It's almost time to go."

"Already?" Neve checked to make sure there weren't any other pages—the book had ended so abruptly, it seemed unfinished—and shivered in spite of the blanket. The day had been strange enough without adding a disturbing book to the mix.

Rose's voice was farther away when she said, "Seriously, let's go. Dad will be here any minute."

Neve slid the paper curtain aside to look out the little window. Rose was staring into the mirror, braiding her hair. Her face was flushed from doing the drills.

"Why does Dad keep taking us?" Neve said. Mom had more free time, Neve thought. Plus, Mom didn't spend every minute in the car discussing whatever they'd just practiced.

Rose met her gaze, then focused back on her braid. "Tennis is important, all right?"

"I know that. I'm just wondering why they're doing it this way. It means Dad has to do a lot more driving."

"Dad gets how important it is, that's why. Mom doesn't. And I want to get good this year."

"You *are* good. You won, like, a ton of matches last season. Did you forget?"

Rose tied off the braid. "You're not getting it either. I want to take it to the next level. Become a serious player."

"I do so get it." Though in truth, Neve didn't. Over the summer they'd had a tournament every other weekend. How much more serious could they get? "You mean you want to do a bunch *more* tournaments."

"Why are you saying it like that? You said you liked them."

"I do like them." They'd been doing the tournaments since Neve was seven and she was used to them. But lately, when she woke up on a Saturday that they *didn't* have one, she felt a little thrill.

"I'm talking about the higher-level tournaments anyway." Rose did a calf stretch off the wall. "I just need to be good at *something.*"

"What do you mean? You're good at everything."

"Seriously? You saw my last math test. I ought to be better than you at math. I'm older." Quad stretches. She pulled on her ankle.

"We can study a little more for math next time. You almost had it."

"Neve, I love how you help me, but I'm not a good student and you know it. I need to start thinking about athletic scholarships for college. And Coach Ellen says now's the time to make plans if I want to get somewhere with tennis. Get more instruction. Really focus on it."

Coach Ellen hadn't said anything to Neve about that. The last suggestion Coach had made to Neve was that she should transfer to a younger practice group where she could be more of a "standout." Neve had *not* thought that was a good idea. "So do that. Practice more. Do all the tournaments. If I don't qualify, I'll still go with you."

"You don't have to do that if you don't want to. And, see, it's not that easy. There aren't even any public courts here . . ." Rose stopped stretching, focused on Neve. "Can you please come out of there? It's hard to have a serious conversation while you're in that thing."

Neve's face grew hot. "Why?" She'd been feeling funny about the boxes since the summer, when Rose's friend Missy Thompson had been in their old room hanging out and asked who the playhouse belonged to. Neve started to tell her it was actually the Mars Rover but Rose interrupted and said it was Neve's *performance art,* the first time Rose had called it that. She had an odd look on her face when she'd said it, though.

"You're in a box, that's why!"

And there was that look again. A look Neve didn't want to ask about because she suspected it meant Rose thought Neve was too old to make these boxes anymore. And if Neve knew *for sure*

28

Rose thought that, Neve would have to stop making them. The box-making was something she'd brought from the old house, something from growing up, a part of her insides that seemed too precious to let go of. "But this is my art. You *said* it was art. Why are you acting like this?"

Rose rubbed her face. "Of course it's art. Don't pay attention to me. Maybe I do need a snack before we go. Or maybe I'm dehydrated. Meet you in the kitchen." The door creaked as she left.

Neve was getting a feeling she'd had most days, if she was being honest, since Rose's thirteenth birthday.

Like she was being left behind.

She climbed out of the box.

Chapter Four

IF NEVE TOLD Dad what Piper had said, it would be like stepping on a yellowjacket nest. He'd be all over them and Mom too.

Though Mom kept saying things like "This was a mutual decision" and "It's been brewing for a while," it was obvious those statements weren't true, at least not from Dad's perspective. Because *he* kept saying things like "This has hit me like a ton of bricks" and "You girls need to tell your mother to come to her senses."

Neve wasn't sure what Dad would do if he heard about Piper's sister, but Neve suspected it would be loud and might involve lawyers, so she didn't want to tell him. It was partly why she hadn't told Rose yet either. *Rose* would definitely tell Dad. Just like she told him what Jody had said the second they got into his car. He hadn't liked it. But scary stories weren't the same thing as a girl's actual disappearance.

Neve mulled it over on the way home that afternoon.

Rose had moved her seat forward so Neve had more legroom in the back of Dad's convertible. The top was down and Neve's ponytail kept whipping her cheeks. They had to talk loudly to be heard.

"Terrific win, Neve!" Dad said, giving her one of his extreme smiles in the rearview mirror. It was always extreme with Dad. It was either *Rob Fenn at your service!* or *Who in the holy hell hid the remote?* Dad burned so bright, it was often nearly impossible to look at him directly.

Rose turned around, and now there were two blue-eyed redheads blasting smiles at Neve. "You rocked it today, sis."

It was an overstatement. Neve had won with a dinky drop shot and a last-minute lob. She tried to smile back.

"Bring some of that get-up-and-go to West Columbia and we'll really have something," Dad said. When Neve didn't respond, he said, "Did you hear me? How will you prepare for that tournament, eh?"

Neve tensed. She couldn't see Dad's entire face in the rearview mirror, but she knew he wore the *Why can't you try a little harder?* expression. *You could be so good, Neve, if you just gave it that extra oomph.* He'd said it before.

"Neve's been practicing a lot," Rose said quickly. "It was her idea to warm up first. By the way, did you see Marsha's warm-up clothes? Bright yellow? What was that all about?"

They were passing a bunch of goats grazing behind a fence. One stared at Neve with those weird slit eyes. *What's your problem?* she wanted to say.

Rose had lied; it hadn't been Neve's idea to warm up. Rose rushed in to defend Neve a lot, really, when Dad was pushing too hard. Neve had told Rose weeks ago that she didn't need to do that anymore, all the *defending*, though she'd said it half-heartedly. Neve wasn't sure she wanted Rose to stop because Dad was pretty hard to ignore. But Rose acted like she didn't know what Neve was talking about anyway.

"Just warming up is not going to cut it," Dad said.

"Neve doesn't need to worry, she's great at tennis," Rose said breezily. "Anyway, I'm thinking we should play at the high school in the spring. Middle-schoolers can play up if they make the team and Jody thinks we'd both make it."

Dad gave Rose a sharp look. "Oh, really?"

Rose glared back at him. Something passed between them that Neve didn't understand. "Neve needs me to be with her," Rose said.

I do, Neve thought. But she didn't say it.

Both Mom and Dad thought they should be more independent. But what *Dad* meant, Neve knew, was that Rose should be independently hanging out with *him* instead of Neve. The secret in Neve's chest rustled around, scratching and digging behind her ribs.

"We'd be able to practice on the high school courts after school," Rose said.

"That's not enough to be a contender and you know it." Dad was back to watching the road ahead. "High school tennis is not where it's at."

Neve didn't agree. High school tennis could be fun. She and Rose could walk to those courts together. They wouldn't need any more rides from Dad back to Acadia Lakes or any more coaching from Coach Ellen, who liked to say Rose was a leader with *so much potential* and Neve needed to *develop her own style.*

But the wind was noisy. The radio was blaring. And Dad and Rose were twinning in looks *and* in volume. The conversation had changed to Rose's complaints about the move and Dad repeating, "No one made your mother move you girls out to the middle of nowhere," reminding Neve of his and Mom's arguments.

Even if Neve had tried to join the conversation — which she wasn't about to — it would have been hard to be heard over all of that.

* * *

Mom could be ruthless when it came to cleanliness.

Neve had kept a lot of the moving boxes to make art projects with, flattening them and hiding them under her bed. But Mom was not having that. Neve managed to save three large boxes but the rest had to go in the trash, Mom said. And the trash pickup was at the street, all the way up the long driveway.

Twilight was creeping in. Neve could see that from the family room. "I'll take them in the morning."

"Now, Neve," Mom said from the kitchen. "The truck comes early."

"I'll get up early." The woods didn't look so friendly this time of day.

Rose painted her nails on the divan. "What's wrong? You're not afraid, are you? Thought you said this was just the country. That I needed to get used to it."

"I'm tired from practice. And it's a long way up there."

But Neve had no choice. And it was even harder to haul the boxes out than she'd expected. The gravel tripped her up and the boxes got heavier as she went. Mom said they were lucky to have curbside pickup and Neve should count her blessings. Instead, she counted steps. She gave up at one hundred.

Finally at the end of the drive, Neve dumped the cardboard and dusted off her hands, then noticed the dog.

A large brown hound. Across the street. He wasn't behind a fence or wearing a collar. Her heart skipped a beat. But the dog didn't rush to sink his teeth into her throat. He simply sat, watching her.

"Nice dog, good dog," Neve said, backing away slowly.

But after a few moments, during which he hadn't come after her, she stopped backing away. She considered him there.

He cocked his head, considering her right back. It made his ears flop. Ears that were comically huge.

Neve laughed. "You *are* a nice dog."

A faint movement. His tail thumped the ground.

She missed dogs. Almost everyone in their old neighborhood had had dogs, and she'd known all of their names.

Neve crossed the street. The hound was larger than she'd first thought. She tried to get closer but he backed up a few paces.

"Are you hungry?" She pulled a leftover granola bar from her pocket and tossed it to him. He gulped it down. "Sorry, it's not much."

She sat on her ankles and he finally ventured over. She scratched behind his ears. The doggy smell of him was strong. "Where'd you come from?" she said. "I didn't think we had any neighbors."

His eyes were the deepest brown, and his droopy eyebrows moved as if he were trying to tell her something. His head seemed huge in comparison to his body; he was thin.

"I think you need more food," she said.

The hound seemed to perk up at the word *food*.

"Wait here." She jogged down the driveway. He didn't follow.

Back at the house, Neve went into the kitchen and filled a bowl with leftover chicken and potatoes.

"What are you doing?" Mom wore yellow gloves and carried a sponge.

"Feeding a dog the size of a small bear."

"Right, sure. Are you feeding the crows again?"

"No wild animals," Rose called from the family room. "It just makes them come around more. I don't want to get eaten by a bear."

"He's not a bear. He's a dog," Neve said, headed to the back door.

"We can't afford to feed the strays, Neve. Let's don't make a habit of this," Mom said.

"Want to come?" Neve said to Rose. "He's one of those big drooly types. You'd like him."

"I bet I would. I just put on the final coat, though." Rose blew on her nails.

Outside, the last rays of orange sunlight stretched across the horizon, and the shadows under the trees had deepened. "It's not that late," Neve said to herself. She jogged, holding the bowl straight out, trying not to spill it. A few minutes later, she set the bowl down in the spot where the hound had been. "Here you go, some food!" Her voice echoed across the empty road. No sign of the hound.

No sign of streetlights either.

Something rustled in the trees. She heard a screech.

Neve's heart leaped in her chest. *Just an owl,* she thought. But she was already running. In the gathering darkness, it was difficult to see where she was going. *I'll probably trip and hurt myself on the gravel,* she thought. No sooner had she thought that than she *did* trip. The fall barely slowed her down, though. She didn't stop running until she was inside. She slammed the door and turned the dead bolt. "Going out at night here. That's a no."

"Must everyone in this house slam doors?" Mom said from the kitchen.

"Got scared, didn't you?" Rose said. "Told you so."

"It's just *really* dark here. It's hard to see."

"Uh-huh. Right. There's a spider hanging over your bed, by the way. It's probably going to bite us in the night."

"There's *not* a spider in your room," Mom called.

Neve gingerly touched her knees, saw beads of blood from her fall. "I don't care about spiders."

"Still," Rose said. "You're not usually afraid of the dark, but here, you don't feel safe. You shouldn't have to feel unsafe in your *own home*."

Neve looked sideways at Rose, whose face was getting red. "I do feel safe."

"Why are we here, anyway?" Rose's voice was rising. "In a place that scares Neve to death?"

"I wasn't scared," Neve said.

"I know why," Rose said, ignoring that. "It's because Mom *chose* to bring us out here. It's a punishment is what it is. One we don't deserve." It was like Rose was auditioning for the school play. She'd give herself a migraine, getting worked up like that.

"I'm okay, really. Don't get upset."

Mom stomped in from the kitchen, smelling of Pine-Sol and gripping a mop as if it were trying to get away. "Rose, please lower your voice. You know very well why we're here. Dad and I are separated and it has nothing to do with you." She glanced at Neve, still standing by the door.

The secret in Neve's chest stabbed. Would Mom come right out and say it, the thing Neve had overheard before they'd moved? "Who's it got to do with, then?"

Mom straightened her shoulders. "No one except your father and me. Rose, don't paint your nails in here. That divan is brand-new."

"Dad said it was your decision to leave. And that you didn't have any reason," Rose said. "We did *not* have to move out here to the middle of bumfrickus."

"If you'd just give it a chance, this could be a time for *all* of us to think about what we want our lives to look like," Mom said.

"I don't need to think about my life. I want to go back home!" They kept fighting.

Neve went into the bathroom to get Band-Aids. She chose the ones with the unicorns, the ones she used to think of as magical. They were buried way down in the bin and were yellowed and stiff. She was too old for them. But it was the kind of night that called for a little magic.

When she came out of the bathroom, the two of them were still fighting. "I'm going boxing, if anyone cares," Neve said.

She ran into the bedroom, grabbed her headphones and tablet, and climbed into her box. Inside, surrounded by cardboard, she could barely hear the fighting. She turned the volume up on her music as loud as she could stand it.

✳ ✳ ✳

Later that night, there was a swishing sound.

Neve was in her box, giving the headphones a rest. Rose had gone into the spare bedroom — the project room, Mom called it — to lie among the stacks of unpacked boxes.

Through the periscope, Neve saw Mom randomly dusting again. She couldn't help herself, it seemed.

Neve pressed two fingers against her chest, holding the secret in place. She took a deep breath. "You missed a spot on the dresser." It was hard work sometimes, distracting Mom from her worrying.

The faintest chuckle. "Oh, you."

"And the desk could use a top-off. A little air freshener, maybe."

"I guess you're right—I'm being silly here."

Now would be the time to talk to Mom about what Piper had said. Rose was likely wearing those earplugs that helped with the headaches and she wouldn't hear them talking. But if Neve told Mom, wouldn't that just make Mom more worried? And what did Neve know, really? She didn't know what exactly had happened. If she mentioned it now, she'd probably just upset them both. She didn't say anything.

"Okay, I'm leaving," Mom said. "Get some rest tonight, will you?"

That night, Neve dreamed of a wild and foamy sea, shadowy creatures swimming in its depths. And when she woke the next morning, she was sweaty, twisted up in her quilt, and not rested at all.

Chapter Five

NEVE SLID into a window seat halfway back on the school bus while Rose sat next to her on the aisle. The dreams of the night before seemed far away as the morning sun warmed Neve's hair.

Rose had styled Neve's hair in a little bun on top, the rest hanging down in gentle waves. Neve preferred it straight, but she knew she needed to follow Rose's advice on this, had known even before the fourth-grade fashion disasters. When Neve was very small, a woman at the grocery store said to Mom, "It's funny how one is so plain when the other is so lovely." Mom had yanked them both away but Neve knew which girl the woman thought was plain.

Plain. Like ice cream without mint or chocolate chips. Neve heard the same sort of things over the years: How she looked like she had no eyebrows. How hopefully she'd grow into her nose. How Mom needed to fatten her up.

"Oh, look. There's the dog," Neve said, focusing out the window. They hadn't seen the hound while they were waiting. But there he was, panting, as the bus drove away.

Rose leaned over Neve to see. "What an adorable dog. He does look like he's starving. I'm glad you brought him food."

The hound's brown eyes were trained on the bus as it rounded the bend. It might look to the dog like the bus was disappearing forever. *We'll be back*, Neve wanted to tell him.

"Speaking of adorable," Rose said. "When that Sammy Garcia gets on, I want you to laugh like you're laughing at something I said."

"Why? Do you like him?"

"I don't *like*-like him, but he's cute, don't you think?"

Neve thought about that. Sammy was in her mutualism group in science class, so she'd gotten a good look. His hair *was* nice, she supposed. Like everyone said. And his smile. He wasn't particularly tall, though he was a point guard on the basketball team. "Yes?"

Rose laughed. "You'll get it soon."

"Okay." Neve smothered a twinge of annoyance. Rose had been talking about boys lately as if she knew something Neve didn't, often using a breathy sort of voice when she mentioned particular ones. But as much as she wanted to, Neve couldn't see anything worth getting breathy over.

The bus began to fill up. Rose chattered, and Neve laughed when she was supposed to. She pulled out her colored pens and the notebook with her drawings.

She had some ideas for a new box design. It would appear to be an automaton, like a music box, she thought, with cutout figures on the top that moved. She'd put a crank on the side, but that would only be for show. Neve would be inside making the figures slide around.

Just for fun, she started to sketch Punch and Judy–type puppets, those old-timey puppets that clubbed each other. Except that on her box, Neve decided, Judy would be the only one doing the clubbing. She'd sketched both figures before she realized that Judy wore a sweatshirt like Mom's, and Punch's jacket had the same pattern as Dad's favorite shirt. She hurriedly turned to a fresh page. Rose wouldn't approve of Neve drawing Mom clubbing Dad over the head. Rose had made it clear she took Dad's side on the separation. But Neve felt Dad shouldn't be making snarky comments to Mom about moving out. Especially as Mom didn't make snarky comments back. Just thinking about it made Neve's chest feel tight.

"Hiya, Sammy," Mrs. Peterson said at the front of the bus.

Sammy returned the greeting and added, "Mom says hi."

He walked down the aisle of the bus toward them and Neve laughed like Rose had told her to.

Rose, clearly aware of what Neve was doing, laughed too.

Sammy slid into the seat in front of them. Big smile. He greeted them both. He and Rose fist-bumped.

"Your mom knows Mrs. Peterson?" Rose said.

"Yeah. Mrs. Peterson's been driving forever," Sammy said. "She was driving when my *mom* went to school here."

Neve glanced up at the driver. Mrs. Peterson wore a trucker's hat with a big plastic knife stuck in it. *Forever* likely included the past two years. That meant she might have been driving when Piper's sister went missing.

While Rose and Sammy continued to talk, Neve went back to sketching. Figures that looked like her and Rose.

The bus pulled up to school. Sammy stood and said, "What-cha drawing?"

Neve showed him.

"Cartooning! Nice." Then this guy Jayden jokingly bumped Sammy's shoulder, distracting him.

"Me and you, playing tennis," Rose said, her voice flat.

"We look cartooned because it's for a box, if that's what you're wondering," Neve said, then worried she shouldn't have mentioned a box. Rose had been weird about the boxes yesterday.

"It *is* nice," Rose said and patted Neve's arm. But she didn't say it in the way Sammy had. She seemed almost sad or like she felt sorry for Neve.

"You don't have to pretend to like it if you don't," Neve said.

"I know that," Rose said. "I didn't mean anything bad. It's brilliant, as always. You're going to be a famous artist one day and I'm going to be a famous actress and I'll come with my entourage to see your art shows."

Neve stood to follow Rose. "But you'll have already seen all my art. Because you'll live next to me."

"That's true. But I'll come to your shows anyway, to be supportive."

Rose high-threed with Mrs. Peterson and stepped off the bus. Neve remembered her thought from earlier and said, "Hold on. I'll be right behind you." She turned to the driver.

"Mrs. Peterson . . ." The plastic knife was made to look like the woman had been stabbed in the head and it was covered in fake blood. It was hard to look at.

"Call me Elvira, girl," the driver said.

Neve took a breath. "Okay, so, Mrs. Elvira, I wanted to ask you about where we live. I heard someone disappeared from there."

The driver's brows came together. "Disappeared?"

"Piper Turner said her sister went missing two years ago. She said she'd lived near us. I thought maybe you drove them."

Mrs. Peterson flinched as if something had stung her. "Good heavens, the Turner girl. I try so hard not to think about it that I'd practically forgotten. It was a long time ago. It's nothing for you to be concerned about."

"But the stories . . . we heard that people think it's cursed out where we live."

"People can get riled up with such nonsense. They want everything to have an explanation. But sometimes things just happen. And the last word I had was that young Miss Turner went to meet her cousin in Georgia. It had nothing to do with the swamp."

"A swamp? What swamp?"

"Way back in the woods over where you live. At least, I've heard there's one back there. But worrying over a swamp is superstitious nonsense. A swamp is just mucky water with bugs and rot and stink. Dime a dozen around here. Go on to school, now."

44

Neve thanked her.

When she stepped off the bus, Rose was waiting with Sammy. She said, "What were you talking to Mrs. Peterson about?" And Neve thought she detected a hint of that *knowing* expression, since Rose was talking to a *boy*.

Sammy, still smiling, raised his brows. He wanted to know too.

Neve *definitely* needed to talk to Piper. "Nothing much," she said.

✳ ✳ ✳

After homeroom, Neve and Rose walked toward their first-period class. Rose was telling a story about clawing her way to victory in a to-the-death tennis match when Neve spotted a girl in a boxy shirt and a red beanie in front of an open locker outside of their language arts class. Piper.

Neve touched Rose's arm. "Can I meet you inside? I want to ask Piper something."

"Um, okay," Rose said, glancing from Neve to Piper and back again. Rose was noting that this was the second time in so many days that Neve had talked to Piper, Neve knew, though she couldn't tell what Rose thought of it.

"It's about something she said at the end of science class yesterday," Neve said.

Rose smiled with what might have been relief and walked into the classroom.

When Neve approached Piper, she didn't look up, though she wasn't getting a book out of the locker. She was just staring into it at a poster that read I LOVE YOU FROM MY HEAD TO-MA-TOES.

"I'm sorry I didn't call last night," Neve said. "We had tennis practice and Mom made me clean up a bunch of stuff. And then it was too late."

A long pause. Then Piper turned in a sudden movement and grabbed Neve's arm. "Meet me in the library at lunch. I'll tell you everything."

Piper's deep green eyes matched the pom on her hat. Though it wasn't actually a pom, Neve realized. It was a stem of felt with two green knit leaves. The hat was designed to look like a tomato.

And Piper was squeezing Neve's arm a little too tightly.

"Um, all right," Neve said. "I can do that."

* * *

The boy in the red shirt showed up right before lunch.

He was in the nook in the hall that might once have held vending machines but now held oversize band instruments or the odd sports bag or field hockey sticks. It wasn't exactly a place for standing.

But there he was, in the shadows, a smaller boy with mussed dark hair that was longer in the front, which made it hard to see

46

his eyes, and ears that stuck out.

Neve felt him looking, and when she looked back, he was smiling at her.

It wasn't, however, a smile that made her feel like smiling back.

It was a smile that made her flinch and walk away and wonder who he was and why he thought it was okay to smile at her like that.

"Hey, where are you going?" Rose said, coming out of the bathroom. "I didn't take *that* long."

"Sorry," Neve said, glancing back at the nook. The boy was no longer there. "This boy was staring at me. I don't remember seeing him before."

"Probably he likes you. That's what they do," Rose said, sipping from her water bottle.

"I don't think so," Neve said. "It wasn't in a nice way. It was more like he wanted something from me. It made me feel a little scared, honestly."

"Where?" Rose said.

"He was there. But he's gone now."

"Point him out to me at lunch. I'll tell him to cut that out. Creeper. We'll report him so fast, it'll make his head spin."

"Yes, okay, but about lunch," Neve said. "I told Piper I'd meet her in the library first. She wants to, um, go over something with me."

"Piper. The girl with the hat, right?"

Neve felt like she needed to explain it. "She really likes tomatoes."

Rose carefully put her water bottle into her backpack. "Yeah, so, Jody says that Piper's a little . . . different. I'm not saying don't be nice to her. You should definitely be nice to her. But I'm not sure she's that great of a friend for you. You should focus on Bets, from math class. So normal and cute. Dad said he could take us to the movies this weekend. What about I invite Jody and you invite Bets?"

Bets *was* cute. An upturned nose, long brown hair. She smiled a lot. "Absolutely, we can do that. I'm not trying to be friends with Piper. It's something for class. I'm sure it won't take the whole lunch period. Save a seat for me, will you?" Neve added a cheerful smile.

Rose blinked. She'd probably expected to be asked to come to the library too. Neve normally would have asked her. But Rose didn't mention it. "Okay. See you in a few."

* * *

In the library, Neve described the boy she'd seen in the hall. "Do you know a boy like that?"

"I can't think of a boy like that, but that's not a whole lot of description to go on," Piper said, moving to sit at the resource computers.

Neve sat next to her and felt embarrassed for making a big

deal of a boy who'd smiled when Piper obviously wanted to talk about something more important.

"Cucumber-stuffed tomato?" Piper had a plastic container full. "No wheat."

"Thanks." While Neve chewed, she thought about the boy. What was it about him that bothered her so much?

"Me and my pops made them. Bubba doesn't like to cook," Piper said. Then added, "I have two dads."

Since Piper seemed to be expecting a response, Neve offered, "Rose's friend Tabitha Summers has two moms. They moved to New Jersey, though."

Piper nodded. "All right, then." She showed Neve a photo album on her phone. Jannie, her sister, had brown hair, unlike Piper's strawberry, though they both had about the same number of freckles, which was a lot. In one photo, Jannie wore a sundress and a Braves ball cap. She held a fat tomato on her palms as if she were offering it to the camera.

"That was from Piper vine," Piper said. "She named it after me. She said those were the best tomatoes she'd ever grown. It's still alive, that vine."

"How old was she?"

"Fourteen." Piper put down her phone and tapped on the computer keyboard. "See, here's the article from the sheriff's department requesting the public's help."

Neve read from the article. "'Investigators believe she may be a runaway.'"

"That's completely wrong. They said that because she'd been talking to our cousin in Atlanta. I talked to him too. They never discussed her going there. She was *gardening*. Who runs away in gardening clothes? She didn't have a cell phone. Or money. I was inside on the couch the afternoon she was taken. I can't believe I was just sitting there reading and eating chips. The chips were her favorite kind too, dill pickle flavor, and I ate the whole bag. On purpose." She rubbed her eyes.

Neve waited. She didn't know what to say.

"And that's it." Piper's eyes were red-rimmed, but she wasn't crying.

"What do you mean, that's it?"

"I mean there aren't any updates. They never found anything. There were never any updates on the others either."

"The others?"

"Yes. There was Morgan Nichols, who was in third grade with me. Also, there was a girl who'd moved here from Bethune four years earlier. The one from Lucknow a few years before that. Go back further and there's more. They didn't find any of them. But I know they're connected."

Neve frowned. She'd never heard of that many kids going missing from one place. "Connected how?"

"I'm not sure yet. But I'm going to figure it out. And when I do, I'm going to *get* whoever or whatever took them. And I'm going to *make. Them. Pay.*" Piper pounded a fist into a palm.

This was what Rose must've meant by *different*. Piper was

focused on finding out what had happened to Jannie, and the other kids didn't get it. Neve thought a better word was *intense*. And Neve, having Rose for a sister, was very familiar with intense. "What do you mean, *whatever* took them?"

Piper stopped pounding her fist. She looked uncomfortable. Then she clicked on the keyboard and pulled up a spreadsheet. A list of the missing girls. There must have been a dozen of them. With details on the locations where they'd gone missing, what they looked like, the people who'd last seen them, quotes from various articles.

"Wow, you've got so much information. How'd you figure all that out?"

"I've had a lot of time on my hands. My dads have barely let me out of the house since Jannie. Bubba even got a different job so he could work from home. But I'm showing you this so you'll understand that I've looked at a lot of possibilities. That I know what I'm doing. That I'm a *professional*."

"Okay," Neve said.

"Think about this too: Missing kids are a big deal, right? Why isn't it news? There's always a lot of attention at first. But then people seem to forget. Not Pops and Bubba, for sure, but everyone else. And there's been so many kids over the years. Why doesn't that get more attention? Special Netflix shows. Journalists coming around. Why do people forget so easily?"

"I don't know." Neve didn't really think Piper was expecting an answer.

Piper took a deep breath. "Hear me out here. On that day, the day Jannie went missing, something happened. Something that made me drop everything and go outside. I didn't put on my shoes or mark my place in my book, and I was right at the part in *Breadcrumbs* where Hazel finds the witch." Piper stared at the computer screen but she wasn't really looking at it. She looked more like she was trying not to cry.

"And?" Neve prompted gently.

"There was a flash of light outside. And a cracking sound. And as soon as I heard it, I knew something bad had happened to Jannie. I knew it like that." Piper snapped her fingers.

"Thunder?"

"It wasn't thunder. It was lower, different. I remember running out the back door, down the steps. The garden was so green. The basket was on the ground with the cabbage and red tomatoes, wisps of fog at the woods. And it was like there was a hole in the world where Jannie should have been. I also felt something else, still there, all around me. I *felt* it."

"Felt what?"

The overhead lights sparkled off the frames of Piper's glasses. "Magic. It was magic that took her. And you can't tell me it wasn't. Because I was there and I know what I felt."

Piper was dead serious. She was.

A whoosh of breath came out of Neve like she'd been punched. She stood. "Oh, will you look at the time? I've got to go. I *promised* I'd meet Rose."

"You don't believe me."

"No, no. It's not that. Rose just needs a lot of help. With math." That was sort of true. Rose usually did need help with math.

Neve got out of there quickly.

The day was just getting stranger.

Chapter Six

ROSE HAD NOT saved Neve a seat at the lunch table.

Or, rather, she had saved Neve a seat, but it was *not* next to Rose. It was on the other side of Bets, whom Rose had apparently invited to sit with them.

Neve was so surprised that she forgot to get a drink or any utensils, so she just sat down with her tray and nibbled a tasteless celery stick while Bets and Jody (who was on Rose's other side) listened to Rose finish a story about this kid Eli in social studies who'd apparently been saying something about Rose's hair. Or something. Neve didn't exactly follow, even though Bets occasionally turned and shook her head at Neve with her eyebrows up in an expression that meant *Isn't this wild?* Neve didn't follow what was being said because Bets was *in her seat,* and no one had taken Neve's seat before, at least not without Rose asking that person politely to scooch over when Neve got there.

The worst part was that Rose didn't seem to notice.

At the end of the period, most of them headed off to math, including Bets and Jody. Neve joined them silently. Though Rose was still telling stories, Neve wasn't listening because she was thinking about what Piper had said and wanted to talk to Rose about it in private. But Neve couldn't, because a bunch of kids were standing closer to Rose than she was.

✳ ✳ ✳

The next time Neve and Rose were alone was on the bus that afternoon after everyone else had gotten off.

"Why didn't you save me a seat?" Neve said. "At lunch?"

"What are you talking about?" Rose said. "I did save you a seat. I even got Bets. Isn't she great? She'll be so fun this weekend. I just know it."

Neve sighed. Rose was pretending she didn't know what Neve was talking about, or maybe Rose actually *didn't* know what Neve was talking about, and that was worse. So Neve moved on to telling Rose about Piper's sister and the other missing girls. Neve also told Rose about the magic.

"Hmm," Rose said when Neve was finished.

"Aren't you upset?" Neve said.

"I already knew about it, pretty much. Jody told me Piper's sister ran away. But Jody didn't know anything else. And she didn't mention any other girls."

"Piper had a spreadsheet with all the girls' names. All this information. What do you think we should do?"

"Did you Google it? Check it out?"

"No—should I?"

"Jody says Piper never got over what happened. Like, it's

55

unhealthy how much she thinks about it. And now you tell me she believes in *magic?*"

"You think Piper made all the girls up? She had so much detail; you should've seen it. Even if she imagined the magic, the girls are still gone."

"Say for a minute Piper's telling the truth, that someone actually took her sister, took a bunch of other girls too. Doesn't that mean Mom brought us to the most terrible place possible? Why would she do that? Is she trying to get rid of us?"

Neve's chest pinched. "She couldn't have known about the girls. Piper says people forget."

"People just forget about missing kids? Not likely. If Mom had done even a smidgen of research before she up and moved us, she would have known about it. No, either it's not true or Mom is a monster."

Neve didn't know what to say to that. Of course Mom was not a monster. Mom worried about them all the time. There must be some other explanation.

The bus was pulling up to their driveway. The hound was there. He seemed to be waiting for them. They stood.

"Mrs. Peterson," Rose said, "have a bunch of kids gone missing here?"

The driver wore a witch's hat decorated with fake spiderwebs and a skull with a gaping mouth. She blinked at them. "Missing kids? I don't recall anything about that."

"But we talked about Piper Turner's sister just this morning," Neve said. "You told me some people blamed a swamp at first."

56

Mrs. Peterson flinched. "Good heavens! The Turner girl. I'd practically forgotten. She ran off, that girl, to see her cousin. These things just happen sometimes. It's nothing for you to be concerned about. Go on home, now."

They stepped off the bus.

"That was weird, right?" Neve said, scratching the hound behind the ears. "She said almost exactly the same thing this morning."

"Didn't seem weird to me. What's weird is you talking to our bus driver about a missing girl and not telling me."

"Sorry. I wanted to talk to Piper more first. I didn't want you to worry if it was nothing. I promise—" And then Neve's face flushed because she would normally have added *no more secrets*, combined with a pinkie swear. It was something they always did, part of making up. But she *couldn't* swear that, not now. Not with the painful thing she was keeping behind her ribs.

Surprisingly, Rose didn't demand *no more secrets* or the pinkie swear. She just shook her head and started down the drive.

Neve let out a breath and followed, the dog trotting behind.

After a minute or two, Rose said, "Magic, huh? You really believe that part?"

"No," Neve said. "Or, well, I believe that's what Piper thinks it was."

"Kinda makes me doubt all of it, gotta admit. Though it was nice of you not to want me to worry."

"We should talk to Mom about it."

Rose nodded. "Yeah. We can do some research on her phone. If Piper's right, Mom's got some explaining to do."

And Neve felt better because at least they had a plan.

But Mom's car was gone again.

"Ugh. And no Dad either," Rose said. Dad was meeting with a client in Columbia, they knew, and wouldn't be taking them to tennis.

Near the back door, the hound sniffed at Mom's planting bed.

"Mom's rosebushes are dying. Poor Mom," Neve said. The bushes Mom had transplanted were curled and brown. She'd planned on the roses blooming in red and white in the spring, but the bushes looked like they'd been poisoned.

"Told you she doesn't know what she's doing. She probably planted them too close together."

The hound's nose went up, pointed across the overgrown yard. A bush shook as if a squirrel was hopping from limb to limb. Except the shaking didn't stop. The dog trotted toward it.

"Should we go see what that is?" Neve said.

"Thought you were just telling me this place is dangerous."

"But this is in the yard. I'll just run over."

"Whatever. I'm going to get a drink of water."

Neve jogged after the hound. She'd look quickly and go back to the house.

In the bush, a small bird was caught in a net. The dog stared up at it, nose quivering.

"Hang on," Neve said to the bird.

It wasn't easy to untangle. The bird's little pointy feet were wrapped in netting, its brown feathers ruffled. It made terrified squeaking sounds. She had to hold it around the middle and could feel its rapid heartbeat. The bird seemed to know what Neve was trying to do, though, and it nipped her only a few times. Finally, she got it loose and it flew away.

"There's a bunch of this netting," Neve said to the hound. The netting was nearly invisible against the branches. She would ask Mom to help her cut it down later.

Neve walked back to the house. The hound waited outside as she stepped through the door. "You know, I think someone was setting traps for birds," she said.

"Look what Mom left this time," Rose said, emerging from the kitchen. "I mean, does she think we are five?" Apples sliced to look like monsters with gelatin for eyes and sunflower seeds for teeth. "Why does she keep being gone and leaving weird food? I can't take this anymore. I'm going running."

Neve followed her into the bedroom. "I thought Mom said you couldn't do that. Not until she figured out what's what around here. You're not allowed."

"Well, la-di-da. Since when are you such a rule follower?" Rose was changing into running shorts.

"Since, like, always. And you've been complaining about this place being creepy since we moved in. And now we hear kids have disappeared. *Why* would you want to run now?"

Rose rummaged in the closet, threw out one running shoe

and then another. "Something is wrong with Piper. I know you've noticed."

"Just because she's into tomatoes doesn't mean she's not right about this. She really believes something might happen to us."

"It would serve Mom right if something did happen. Bringing us to this horrible place. Making us stay inside when I desperately need fresh air. Are you really, truly, all that worried?" Rose paused in tying her shoes.

Neve remembered the frightened bird, its little heart beating fast. "There was a bird trap. Who would have set it? There's no one around here. Don't you think that's a tiny bit odd?"

Rose rolled her eyes. "It was probably just some old netting. Listen, I won't go far. And besides, nothing bad happens in the daylight on a nice day."

Neve didn't answer. Sometimes bad things *did* happen in the daylight. Piper's sister had been gardening in the afternoon. Neve followed Rose into the kitchen.

"Here's the part where you say you'll go with me," Rose said, filling her water bottle. "That a run would do you good. And you can keep an eye on me."

It was the type of statement Neve *would* make. Because Rose usually talked her into everything. "No. I won't go and you shouldn't either."

"What is wrong with you?" Rose said. "Why are you being so stubborn?"

"Well, why aren't you listening to me? I know we don't have

all the facts, but I've got a feeling there's something to the stories we've heard. Piper seems believable. The bus driver was acting strange. And remember that boy I saw?"

"Leave it to Neve to be upset because a boy *smiled* at her."

That stung because Neve wasn't all that comfortable with boys and Rose knew it. "Piper had a *list* of missing girls," Neve said. "They *haven't been found.*"

"Piper is still upset about her sister. That makes sense. And sure, it's weird and creepy here, but we haven't seen anything that's actually dangerous. You're getting me upset over nothing. Over *magic*. Giving me migraines for *no reason.*" Rose's face was getting red.

"*I'm* giving you migraines?" Neve rubbed her chest where it ached. "No, you're making *me* upset, going running in a place that's dangerous."

"Maybe I should move back in with Dad if I'm so much trouble, hmm?"

Neve's mouth fell open. "You would do that?"

"Oh, grow *up*, Neve. Things don't stay the same forever. It's like you're stuck. All those boxes. I don't want to be stuck here with you."

"*Stuck* with me?"

"I didn't mean it like that. I meant, it's like you're not moving forward. I need to move forward."

"And moving forward is moving back in with *Dad*? Fine. Go ahead! Move back in with Dad."

"Maybe I will!" And without another word, Rose marched out the door and slammed it.

Neve stared at the back door. Then she ran into her room and threw herself into her box.

Chapter Seven

ONCE UPON A TIME, before the founding of the nearby town of Etters, the woods around the swamp had teemed with life. Boars, foxes, deer, birds of all kinds. That was because the animals had not yet learned to be wary of the swamp. They had not yet become afraid of the woman who lived there.

The woman who called herself Mrs. Katch.

Back in those days, it had been easy for Mrs. Katch to take what she needed. And Mrs. Katch needed quite a lot, for her spells were greedy things. But the trees were snitches, passing warnings to the wind. These days, what she needed was getting harder to find.

She'd had to get creative: Nets to catch migrating birds. Clover to attract the rabbits (who were often too stupid to read the wind anyway). And the flexibility to make use of the varied selection of unwanted pets that people seemed to feel no remorse about dumping in the deserted countryside where they were unlikely to be found by anyone *other* than Mrs. Katch.

However, Mrs. Katch's most clever innovation by far was a lure for the magical foxes. She'd had to hand-raise the minnows in a wooden barrel and determine just the right amount of elixir and enchantments, but the trial and error had been worth it. The foxes found the minnow lure irresistible.

Mother had discovered the swamp. But as was typical of Mother, she never truly understood it, never knew the types of things that made it hum.

That afternoon, in the shadows of the cypress, Mrs. Katch stood on a stone bridge, the swamp below covered in a lazy mist. She held a pearl that glowed with the purest light. The size of an acorn and still wet with gore and blood from the latest luckless fox, the pearl would cover the price and then some.

She dropped the pearl into the swamp and, as the water rippled below, she read aloud from a small book bound in worn green leather. The language it was written in was rarely heard today, but she spoke it well enough. Echoing her words were whispers from the book itself.

After she finished reading, Mrs. Katch added, somewhat impatiently, "You know the one I want."

A faint reply from the swamp in what sounded like many voices combined, voices that came from dozens of places within the water: *We accept.*

Mrs. Katch waited, and, sure enough, the mist began to gel and thicken, gradually absorbing the water below until it became a dense white fog, the muck and bones in the swamp bed laid bare.

The swamp was the fog. The fog was the swamp. They were

one and the same. Mrs. Katch had learned that. And what a useful thing that knowledge had proved to be.

The fog was departing. Riding the wind and unspooling itself, the fog wormed its way out of the swamp, passing like a great serpent through the bramble and out to the tall slender pines.

It would not fail to bring her what she wanted.

It never had.

Chapter Eight

THE FAIRY-TALE BOOK was in the box with Neve. Beneath the blanket.

"Oh, that book." She yanked it out and threw it against the side of the box.

She could feel the book lying there resentfully. *Look here*, it seemed to say. *Look at me.*

"I'm *not* looking," she said.

But after a minute or two, she grumpily turned on the book light.

The book had fallen open to the page with the text: *The dwarves came and took the daughter away.* The illustration was a dwarf with a long white beard, wearing tall black boots and a green hat, with a sack slung over his shoulder. A girl's head stuck out of the sack; she was looking back at two small girls chasing after her in their bare feet.

Neve stared at the page for a full minute.

Then she got out of the box. She changed into running clothes and found her shoes.

"I decided to go for a run too. So what? You think you own the road?" she practiced.

Once dressed, she stepped out the back door and there was the hound, dashing toward her. He panted hard, like he'd been trying to keep up with Rose.

I know how you feel, Neve thought.

When he arrived at her feet, he didn't want scratches, didn't want to be petted. He started to run up the drive again, then turned back and looked at her as if to say, *Come on!*

"Yes, I'm going for a run. Because that's the kind of thing I do," Neve said. It wasn't quite the truth. She ran only if Rose decided to, and she usually stopped before Rose did and waited for her to finish.

She jogged slowly, trying not to turn an ankle on the gravel. There was a break in the clouds, and the sunlight reflected off the lake. A woodpecker made a *skritt* somewhere. A gentle wind rustled the leaves of the trees. Leaves that were turning colors. Russet red, burnt orange, a deep yellow.

Maybe Rose was right. It was a nice day. It was a long while before dark. It would all be fine.

When Neve neared the top of the drive, Rose jogged by. She'd obviously been running one way and had turned around. Her doubling back meant she wasn't quite as comfortable as she had pretended to be.

"Rose!" Neve said.

Though Rose was close enough to hear, she didn't answer.

Neve turned onto the road, staying on the shoulder. Rose jogged well ahead, headed north, flanked by the woods. The hound ran in the space between Neve and Rose, big ears flopping.

A wind came just then, and leaves skittered across the pavement. The sun went behind a cloud, casting the road in shadow. Along with the scent of the pines, the wind carried the smells of damp moss and musty earth.

They really needed to get back before Mom did. She'd be so upset if she discovered they'd gone out.

"You should turn around," Neve said. "It's going to rain!"

Rose was still ignoring her.

Neve kept running.

The air started to feel misty, clammy against her skin. A low fog was rolling in. It stole through the trees ahead, wormed its way along the ground, twined around fence posts.

The hound bayed for some reason. Neve had never heard him make any noise before. It was a mournful sound.

Up ahead, a gutted house, the frame rotten, broken glass in the windows, all signs of habitation overtaken by the forest. Neve had seen empty houses before. Still, the sight was sobering. Who had lived there? Where had they gone?

"Come on, Rose!" Neve said.

"Forget it, I'm not talking to you!"

The fog ahead was getting heavier, the fence posts consumed by it.

"Don't be a jerk!" Neve said. Her side hurt. She was getting a cramp.

"You're the jerk. You're not even listening!" Rose came to a stop and turned around, putting her hands on her hips.

When she did, the fog that had been meandering on the roadside suddenly surged toward them, spreading like a flood. It covered Rose's legs, rising to her knees. The sound of faint voices came with it, like a distant crowd. And oddest of all, the fog sent up a feeler that curled around Rose's torso.

The feeler was like nothing Neve had ever seen. Made of fog but resembling a rope . . . "Look out!" Neve said, and the hound was baying.

The flood of fog was rising—up to Rose's waist, her chest, her throat. The sisters' eyes met. The world slowed down until there was nothing but Rose's scream: "Neve!"

A brilliant flash and a loud crack, and the fog engulfed Rose. Then the whole of the fog split down the middle and flowed away.

The hound reached the spot first. And then Neve was there too. In the place where Rose had just been.

The fog was clearing out, retreating back into the trees, back into the forest. The clouds moved away from the sun. The shadows dissolved. The street was bathed in light.

Rose was nowhere to be seen.

* * *

With her screams echoing in the trees, Neve turned in a circle, trying to look in every direction at once, making herself dizzy.

Except for her and the hound, the street was deserted. The fog had gone back into the woods and taken Rose with it.

The only thing left was a shoe. Just one of them, bright orange with a yellow lace, on the asphalt where Rose had just been. People didn't leave their running shoes behind and walk in their sock feet on the road or through woods where there were thorns, rocks, fire ants. They just didn't.

The fog had taken Rose, swept her away, disappeared her, and left only the shoe. How could that be?

Neve picked up the shoe; the lace was still double knotted. She hugged it to her chest. "Rose?" she said, her voice catching. A feeling like static electricity filled the air, flickers of energy she could almost see. The hairs on her arms stuck straight up.

The hound was still baying. He'd been baying since it'd happened.

Crows cawed from the trees and flew up in a burst.

"Bring her back!" Neve shouted to the crows, the fog, the trees.

Her voice echoed: *Back . . . back.* Who did she think she was talking to? What she thought she'd seen could *not* have just happened. People didn't get swept up by fogs.

"Rose, where are you?" she said. "Are you fooling around?"

No sign of Rose in the trees. She'd had on pink Nike shorts. They were practically neon. Surely Neve would've noticed if Rose had bent low, dashed into the trees, was at that moment giggling behind a bush.

But Rose was not a practical joker. And Rose's voice when she'd called out for Neve, when she'd been inside the fog — Rose had been *scared*. The way the fog had coiled around her. The Weather Channel had never shown anything like that. Neve shivered.

The hound was there. He pressed his cold nose into her hand.

"You saw it too," Neve said. "What *was* that?"

He had no answers. He shivered right along with her.

"We shouldn't have come out here. I knew we shouldn't have." Neve turned in a circle again. Which direction had Rose gone?

A car's engine. On the road, coming toward Neve. The Volvo. Mom.

The driver's-side window rolled down. Mom took one look at Neve, stopped the car in the middle of the street, and jumped out, leaving the engine running, the door wide open. She grabbed Neve by the shoulders. "My God, Neve, what is it? What's wrong? Where's Rose?"

Neve burst into tears.

***

Neve sat on the divan in the family room holding a single running shoe. The lights were on. It was dark outside.

"There must've been a struggle," the detective said. Detective Rogers was his name. A lean, tired-looking man, he sat in one of the new rounded armless chairs and seemed unsure of where to put his elbows. "To have thrown off her shoe. She must've fought. Are you sure you didn't see any of that?"

Mom was next to Neve, her arm around her. Dad paced the room.

"The fog slipped over her like a rope," Neve said. "Or a snake. She didn't see it coming. She didn't have time to fight it."

"Uh-huh," Detective Rogers said. He exchanged glances with the uniformed officer, who perched awkwardly in the matching chair.

The uniformed officer mouthed, *Shock.*

They meant her, Neve thought. They thought she was in shock. But *shock* meant staring at nothing with your mouth open. Neve wasn't doing that. She was talking. She was being perfectly logical. They simply weren't listening to what she said.

Dad didn't stop his pacing. "Did you see any people? Anyone at all? *Think*, Neve."

Detective Rogers said to Neve, "It would be helpful if there was something—" He suddenly moved to hold a knee with his clasped hands, like a stretch. It didn't look comfortable.

"Crows. A bunch of them. The hound. A car hadn't passed in a while. Also, there was that bird and the trap." Neve directed her answers to the detective. He was calmer than Dad.

"That it?" Detective Rogers said. "Take your time. Anything more about the feeling like electricity?" He gave up on the chair and rose to lean against the wall.

"That's all I can remember."

"Downed wires?" Detective Rogers said to the uniformed officer, who was still gamely attempting to sit comfortably in the chair.

The uniformed officer nodded. He had a pad and pen. "Was your sister wearing a jacket?" he asked Neve.

"No, just the Nike shorts and that white tank. Oh, and she had a purple hair tie and a water bottle, a metal one, the kind you hold while you run."

The uniformed officer wrote something down on the pad.

"Is there anything you remember her saying?" Detective Rogers said. "Any indication she may have been planning this? Had she been communicating with anyone on the internet?"

"I told you, she never did. We don't even have internet here yet."

"Anything else? This is all good."

"The fog. It had thinned out a whole bunch. But what was left seemed to creep back into the trees. Like maybe it was going somewhere with her."

"Creeping fog," the uniformed officer said. "Going some-where. Uh-huh."

"Yes, you mentioned that." Detective Rogers looked more tired than ever. "I think we're done here," he said to Mom. "Let us know if she remembers anything else. We'll be searching around the property." He took a roll of Tums from his jacket pocket.

Neve had a sudden thought. "What about the list Piper

Turner has? You'll be investigating that list, right? The cases of the other missing girls."

"I don't know who Piper Turner is," the detective said, chewing on a Tums. "But we'll definitely look for patterns across similar cases. And needless to say, we'll need to search your former residence too." He gave Dad a casual glance.

Dad stopped his pacing. "Why would you need to do that?" He turned to Mom.

Beside Neve, Mom stiffened. She didn't say anything.

"In light of your recent action," Detective Rogers said, "it seems best." The detective's glance hadn't actually been casual, Neve realized. A laser focus was behind it.

"You didn't," Dad said. That was to Mom.

"I thought they should know." Mom's tone was clipped.

"What action?" Neve said.

"Now they're going to think I took her," Dad said, "and they'll stop looking where they ought to be looking."

"Don't do this," Mom said. "Let them follow their process."

"Why are you so agitated, Mr. Fenn?" Detective Rogers said.

Dad ran a hand through his hair. That red hair, the color so much like Rose's. Only his had gray in it. His face was also flushed like Rose's often was. "I'm not agitated. You can look through the house all you want. But she's not at her old house."

"You're certain about that?" Detective Rogers said.

"Yes. Well, no. But if she is, *I* didn't put her there," Dad said.

"You're suggesting someone else put her there?" Detective Rogers said.

"I'm not suggesting anything except that you find her like you're supposed to."

Neve's head ached, especially between her eyes. Nothing was making sense. Why were they talking about something Dad had done? They ought to be out on the road looking for Rose in the spot where she'd disappeared. Looking for clues.

Neve eyed Dad. Maybe it was because the police already *knew* something. Maybe they'd discovered evidence they hadn't yet revealed. Maybe they already had a *prime suspect* and were waiting for him to break down and admit his guilt.

Dad paced some more. He wore his salesman striped button-down and tie but he didn't have on his salesman smile. He sold high-end air-conditioning units and was pretty good at it. That meant he was smart, plenty smart.

Mom was saying something. Then the detective.

Neve's heart pounded. Dad was always wanting Rose to be with him. Maybe he'd taken matters into his own hands. Mom had moved Rose to the middle of nowhere, forcing Dad to drive the forty minutes each way. He was retaliating with a devious plan to kidnap Rose. The more Neve thought about it, the more it made sense. Maybe Dad's plan had included . . . a fog machine! A fog machine to cover his tracks. He'd swooped in, grabbed Rose under cover of the fog. His getaway car must've been hidden in the woods.

"Did you do it? Did you take her?" Neve said to Dad.

Mom sucked in a breath. The room quieted. Eyes focused on Neve.

"No!" Dad said.

Detective Rogers gripped the back of a chair. "Is there something you haven't told us?" he said to Neve.

"No . . ." Neve said.

"Why would I do that? Why would I *need* to do that? It's not even logical," Dad said.

"It is logical if you're getting desperate," the detective said.

"Desperate?" Dad repeated. "I'm not desperate. We're working it out."

"That's not what your wife said—"

"I did say our lawyers were working on it," Mom interrupted. "But this is too much for a child to process. Is there anything else you need from Neve? She should go to bed."

I'm not a child, Neve thought.

Detective Rogers didn't answer because he was arguing with Dad. The words seemed to float over Neve's head. The uniformed officer had heard Mom, though. He got the detective's attention and motioned to Neve in a way that the detective seemed to understand.

"We're going to need that shoe," Detective Rogers said. "Could be some physical evidence on there. Evidence of the perpetrator. Too bad she picked it up."

The uniformed officer had gloves, a plastic baggie. He came toward Neve.

There was a lot Neve didn't understand about the current situation: What had happened to Rose. Why they wouldn't listen to her about the fog. What Dad's recent action had been.

But she did understand this. They wanted the shoe.

Neve looked down. The fingers of both her hands were tight around Rose's running shoe. "No," she said.

"Honey," Mom said gently. "It's important to give that shoe to the police."

"I found it," Neve said. "It's mine."

"Give it to the police," Dad said. "Don't you want them to find your sister?"

"I won't," Neve said.

"You've got to, honey." Mom held tight to Neve's arms.

The uniformed officer pried Neve's fingers off the shoe. That officer might have gotten kicked by her. Dad definitely did. Neve was screaming the whole time.

While Mom held her down, the shoe went inside the plastic bag. The uniformed officer sealed it shut. Took it away.

Neve could hear herself screaming and knew she sounded ridiculous. But she couldn't stop.

They were taking the shoe. They shouldn't be taking it.

Dad had to haul her out of the room like she was a toddler, Mom trailing behind. By then Neve was sobbing. It was all just too much. It was all so wrong and too much.

The shoe coming out of her hand had brought it all back: The feel of the road beneath her feet, the sound of her heartbeat in her ears, the misty air filled with shadows. The way the fog had spilled out onto the street, how that tentacle had wrapped around Rose. The baying of the hound. And Neve herself, running as fast as she could, stretching her legs, pumping her arms, her lungs burning. It hadn't been fast enough. Rose's expression in that last second, when it was clear the fog was up to something, her eyes wide as she called out for Neve . . .

"Nooooooo!" Neve shouted now.

She was in her bedroom, inside her box, wrapped in a blanket wet with her tears. Mom and Dad had gone back out to talk to the officers, to explain that their daughter had lost it. That she was overwhelmed. That her perfect logic had gone out the window.

They shouldn't have taken the shoe.

***

Neve huddled inside the box. It was late but the bedroom light was still on. That was because Rose would need it to see by. When she came home.

When the bedroom door opened, Neve looked out the periscope.

Mom's thighs. She wore sweats. Her old jacket.

"Are you in there?" Mom said.

"No," Neve said. "I've gone with Rose's shoe as evidence."

"I'm sorry we had to take it. I really am. But don't you want them to do everything they can to find her?"

"Maybe they should take Dad in as evidence."

"He's on the divan, trying to rest for a minute. That should be evidence enough of his good intentions. Honey, do you want to come out of there? You can sleep in my room. There's going to be more people coming. They'll probably need to look in here."

"I'm too old to sleep in your bed." It wasn't exactly the case. Neve sometimes crawled into the bed with Mom if she was feeling upset. But there was something magic about being in her box. Something that made it seem like wishes could come true.

"Can I get you something to eat? Are you hungry? What's this here?"

Neve slid the paper curtain aside. Mom had picked up the fairy-tale book. Neve had thrown it out of the box earlier. "It's the book you left for me," Neve said. "I hate it, by the way."

"I didn't leave it. Maybe it was still here from the prior owners." She set it on the desk.

"It was the fog, Mom," Neve said. "Why don't you believe me?"

"I *do* believe that's what you saw. We just don't know what else was at play here. Please keep an open mind, honey. It could be something we haven't considered."

"Rose didn't run away." Neve had heard that possibility being *considered* several times by Mom and Dad, rather loudly. And she'd heard Dad accusing Mom numerous times of bringing them to a dangerous place. "I *told* you she didn't run away."

"We just want to find her. Same as you. Now, Dad's going out with the searchers again, but don't worry, we're taking turns and I promise we won't leave you here alone."

"I don't care about that. I want to look too."

"Not until we know more. Call for me if you need anything."
The door creaked as Mom left.

"What I need is Rose back," Neve said to no one.

It was her fault that Rose was missing. All her fault.

The secret scratched inside Neve's chest. It felt big and over-whelming just then, like it might claw its way out of her body, burst out in a spray of blood and shattered bone. She focused on her breathing.

As it turned out, Neve stayed in the box all night, wrapped in the blanket.

She dreamed of Rose.

Neve was on the ground, a baby bird, flopping around. Rose was a bird too, but she was soaring high above, so high in the clouds Neve could barely see her.

"Please," Neve said. "Tell me what to do!"

Rose's return shout was faint. But Neve could swear she heard: "Find the dog."

Chapter Nine

THE HOUND WAS there the next morning.

Neve was out on the road, walking where Rose had disappeared. The sun hadn't been up long, and dew was still on the weeds. She'd left the house before Mom woke up. Dad had been snoring on the divan. They had been up late into the night, Neve knew, taking turns walking around with flashlights with the police, and they hadn't been sleeping long, so she had tried not to wake them.

The hound nudged her leg.

"There you are." Neve scratched behind his ears. "The only other one who saw. What do you think it was, that fog?"

Looking into the hound's deep brown eyes, she could see that he knew something, something he understood without words. Neve felt sure of it.

Another thing Neve felt sure of: Dad hadn't taken Rose. In the clear light of morning, Neve knew that. If he had, why would he still be here? He'd be halfway to Arizona by now, or wherever it was parents who stole their children ran off to. And where would he have plugged in a fog machine? Those machines needed electricity. It had been a ridiculous thought. Last night had just been so upsetting. There'd been so many statements flying around.

Dad's *recent action.*

Stop, she told herself. She couldn't think of that now. That'd been the problem last night: She'd let herself get distracted when she should've stayed focused. If only she'd kept talking, describing the fog in more detail, exactly what it had looked like, acted like. She should have stayed calm until they listened. Until someone hit on a way what she'd seen could've happened. *Oh yes, the northern tundra fog has people-carrying properties! It must have infiltrated our area. We should have thought of that at once!*

Instead, she'd acted like a baby about a shoe. No wonder the police hadn't taken her seriously.

She walked a few paces more. "The shoe was right here. Or maybe over there." The hound followed her.

Nothing there but asphalt, of course. The late-night team had checked everything out while Neve had been hiding in her box.

Neve surveyed the area. Fragile clouds across a pale morning sky. A pair of officers searched around the lake. The gold badges on their uniforms glinted through the trees. The cruiser had been up by the road when she left the house.

A bus passed her and parked on the street. On its side: MIRACLE SPRING CHURCH. Old people started getting out. Volunteers there to search. Mom said they'd be coming.

There were a lot of places to search: the house, the driveway, the yard, the stretch of highway, and the endless woods.

"I don't know where to start," Neve said. "We should try and eliminate some places. Any thoughts on narrowing it down?"

The hound sniffed her hand, likely checking to see if she had any food, then went off to inspect something in the weeds, nose to the ground, tail up. His posture gave Neve an idea.

"That's right. You're a *hound* dog. Hound dogs can sniff anything out. Let's go get something of Rose's. We can get started right away."

She dashed down the driveway toward the house. He followed, loping behind.

She burst through the back door.

Mom was standing right there. She ambushed Neve in a hug. "Darling."

"Mom," Neve protested. "I'm busy here."

"Where have you been? I was just coming to look for you. What are you doing sneaking out? You cannot be out of the house right now. It's too dangerous."

"What? I didn't sneak."

Dad stood in the family room, wearing the same shirt from yesterday, untucked and wrinkled. A scruff of beard growth on his cheeks, his glasses crooked. His hair stuck up. "There's a kidnapper on the loose."

"We don't know that." Mom gave him a frustrated look. "But we can't be too careful."

"Mom, I'm going to give a hound dog something of Rose's, like one of her shirts. He can sniff her out."

"It's the right idea," Dad said. "But search and rescue's going to be here within the hour. Those bloodhounds are trained. They have handlers."

"Our dog could find her," Neve said. "Let's give him a chance."

"No," Dad said. "He might mess up the trail for the officers. Where'd that dog come from, anyway?"

"I think he's a stray. And I think we should keep him," Neve said.

"We can worry about the dog later," Mom said. "Right now we can't have you wandering around. It's far too risky."

"But I need to do something," Neve said. "I can't sit around here not helping."

Mom exchanged a glance with Dad. "We know that."

"You need to go to school," Dad said.

"School? Why would I do that?" Neve said, her voice rising.

"Please, honey, we need for you to be safe," Mom said. "We can't look out for you today. There's going to be a lot happening. A lot of people here. You're safest at school."

"Let Grandpa come," Neve said. "He can watch me."

"You know Grandpa can't travel by himself anymore," Mom said.

Dad said, "Look, you need to cooperate. We can't be dealing with you on top of everything else."

"Rob, please," Mom said. "Neve, hear me out. We'll call the school the second we know anything. The bus will be here soon. Let me comb out your hair, darling. And have you eaten?"

"I don't want to eat anything," Neve said. "And I am *not* getting on that bus."

✳ ✳ ✳

Neve did get on the bus.

Or, to be more precise, Dad put her on the bus. Neve was not being very cooperative. Being uncooperative was becoming her thing.

Mrs. Peterson — in a Mad Hatter hat — sighed as she pulled the bus door shut. "What's happened, girl?"

Neve couldn't answer. She was afraid she'd burst into tears. Plus, she'd managed to cut her lip on her braces while struggling with Dad. She could taste the blood. She shrugged and retrieved her backpack from the bus steps. Dad had tossed it in after her. "Chin up," he had said.

"Sit you down right there." Mrs. Peterson indicated the seat behind her.

Neve sat.

"Put your hand in that jar," Mrs. Peterson said.

A plastic jar with no lid was duct-taped to the back of Mrs. Peterson's seat. It was filled with peppermints. Neve took one out.

"Good girl. Now, you put that candy in your mouth and you

suck on that until we get to school. Sometimes a soul just needs a candy."

"Thank you, Mrs. Peterson."

"Call me Elvira."

No one sat next to Neve. Mrs. Peterson wouldn't let them. When Sammy got on and said hey to Neve, Mrs. Peterson said, "Girl is having some quiet time right now." That was code for someone being in trouble. Sammy's eyebrows went up. And Neve got some interested looks from the other kids.

I don't care if they think I'm a troublemaker. It kept Neve from having to talk to anybody, which she didn't think she could handle.

The streets, the houses, everything passed by in a blur.

✳✳✳

Neve didn't notice Piper in the hallway until she was right in front of her.

"I know what happened." Piper wore her tomato hat.

"You do?"

"The police are in the front office talking to the administration. They'll want to talk to the teachers next. Then some students. Everyone in the school is going to know within the hour."

"How do you know all that?"

"I listen. I pay attention. Also, I had to drop off a note in the office and I heard them mention Rose. I checked WIS News online. The sheriff's department has already got it on there."

"I'm too upset to talk about this right now."

"Now's *exactly* the time to talk about it. So we can find her before it's too late. And was it . . . was it the magic? Is that what we're looking at here?" Piper was staring at Neve as if they had something in common. It made Neve frown.

"No, this was different," Neve said. "It was fog. The police are going to figure out about the fog." That wasn't true, of course. The police hadn't listened to her about the fog.

"Fog? You think it was fog? All right, then. Meet me in the library at lunch," Piper said. "We can work on a strategy."

Neve did not want to work on a strategy with someone wearing a tomato hat. Neve knew about fantasy. She liked fantasy too. But fantasy was not going to bring her sister back.

"Listen," Neve said. "I'm sorry about your sister, but this is real life and not some book you're reading."

It came out harsher than she'd intended. Piper's face fell and she jerked away.

"Wait!" Neve called after her.

But Piper didn't turn around.

* * *

Piper had been right. The curious looks started by second period. People *knew*.

And since Rose was already known to every person in the

school, or so it seemed, there were a lot of looks. The owners of those looks—many of them, anyway—tried to talk to Neve. They asked her what had happened. Wide eyes, exaggerated whispers, touches on her sleeve. *Are you okay?*

"I don't know," Neve replied to the questions about what had happened. And obviously, she was *not* okay. She didn't bother to answer those questions. All the other questions just looked like mouths moving. The faces blurred, the names a jumble.

She went numb, walking the hallways with a ghost next to her. Occasionally, she would space out for a moment and turn to ask Rose if she'd remembered her book for social studies or if she thought Neve's hair looked okay or if she could believe that they had to read three chapters for English by tomorrow.

But of course, Rose wasn't there, and Neve's insides would go hollow as it all came flooding back, and she'd nearly pass out right there in the hallway.

✳ ✳ ✳

In math class, Mr. Adams droned on about rational-number word problems. It was material Neve had already learned in her old school. But even if she hadn't, there was no way she could pay attention. She stared at the Halloween-themed bulletin board: *Don't Be Scared, It's Only a Math Problem!*

This was a problem like any other. Neve just needed to figure out the method for solving it. But it made her head ache. Maybe she was getting a migraine, like Rose.

Mom said stress caused Rose's headaches. Maybe that was why Neve was getting one. It was certainly stressful to have your sister missing. Though Neve had never gone missing. She had been right there each and every day. So what had Rose been so stressed over?

Neve. Neve actually being there was giving Rose migraines. Rose had said Neve wasn't *listening*.

Neve rubbed the place between her eyes. She had to get Rose back before she worried about that. And to get Rose back, Neve had to *think*. Since Mom and Dad had forced Neve to be at school, surely there was a way to do something from here.

Neve looked at Rose's empty desk. If she could, she would ask Rose what to do. Because what would Rose do if the situation were reversed?

An image quickly came to mind: Rose marching around, a finger pointed in the air, her hair in a business-like bun. Neve could practically see her. Rose would be *demanding* that her sister be returned. She would not be listening quietly to Mr. Adams. She'd be doing something. Several somethings. And the somethings Rose would be doing would be loud. They would get noticed. They would be heard.

But *what* would Rose do, exactly? Neve closed her eyes. She pictured writing a note and passing it over to an imaginary Rose when Mr. Adams wasn't looking.

While Neve waited, imaginary Rose unfolded the note.

Imaginary Rose made a face at the mention of magic fog—*Seriously, Neve?*—then imaginary Rose scribbled madly on the note.

Organize a big search party! Insist on a press conference! Make stores put up missing-person posters!

Those were the types of things Rose would do. Those were the types of things Rose would want *Neve* to do.

Neve opened her eyes. She got out her drawing notebook, found a fresh page, and, with three different color gel pens, wrote the things down. Then she added a bunch of underlines and stars. She would do this. She would.

She would find Rose herself.

Chapter Ten

NEVE JUST NEEDED to show everybody she was serious, like Rose would be.

When math class was finally over, Neve twisted her hair into a tucked-under bun and marched up to Mr. Adams.

He was shuffling papers.

She waited.

"Oh, I'm sorry, Neve," Mr. Adams said after a moment. "I didn't see you there. Can I help you?"

"My sister's missing."

"I know. Everyone cares for your sister so much. I hope you realize that." He ran a hand through his hair, as he often did. It didn't help the helmet hair he had from riding his bike to school.

"I want to organize a search party. There's a ton of land around my house. The police can't search it all."

"Sounds like that's what needs to be done. But several groups are already organizing, aren't they?"

"Yes, but I want to get kids and teachers to come from the school, on the buses, right away."

"Ah, well, I'm not sure. I think you have to have some

search-and-rescue training? But Mrs. Tish coordinates the buses for the field trips. If you want, I could talk to her."

Rose would not have waited for Mr. Adams to do it, Neve thought. "Thank you. I'll go talk to her myself." Neve marched out of the room. She stopped at her and Rose's locker to put on one of Rose's cardigans and some of Rose's pink lipstick, for luck, then headed to the wing that housed the art classroom. Mrs. Tish was the art teacher.

Mrs. Tish was tacking up a row of paintings by the sixth-graders. The kids must've all had the same assignment: a road into a dark wood. The paintings were many different versions of the same gloomy road.

Neve told the teacher what she wanted.

"What a splendid suggestion," Mrs. Tish said. "Why *shouldn't* we use the buses for that? Why *shouldn't* we go during the day? We can all pitch in to help find her. Let me see. We'll need to get transportation forms signed. And Principal Williams's permission. The kids will need to wear pants because of briars . . . my goodness, it just breaks my heart about Rose. I'll get everything together and bring it to the staff meeting this afternoon. We might could get out there tomorrow."

"Tomorrow?" Neve felt a crushing disappointment. "But I wanted everyone to go today. She's been gone since yesterday."

"Oh, sweet girl, I don't think that'll be possible. Not with middle-schoolers and the permissions we'll need to get. But I like the way you're thinking. Don't lose heart. I'll tell you what—I'll keep working this angle, but you should go straight to the top.

Talk with Principal Williams. She might have some other ideas. Go on, now. Tell her I sent you."

Though the bell was already ringing, Neve ran down the hall to the front desk. The desk held plastic violets, a sign-in sheet, and a motivational sign: YOU CAN HAVE RESULTS OR EXCUSES. NOT BOTH!

She took a breath. "Can I talk to Principal Williams?"

"What'd you say, hon?" Miss Terry, the secretary, asked.

Speak up, Neve. It was something Dad often told her. *Be more assertive.* She repeated the question, louder.

"You're the girl whose sister is missing, aren't you?" Miss Terry said.

Neve nodded.

"Hold on a minute, please." The secretary rolled her wheelchair over to the door of the principal's office and explained the situation.

"Send her in," the principal said.

Neve walked into the principal's office. She took a deep breath and told her about her ideas.

"Mrs. Tish was right," Principal Williams said when Neve finished, "to send you my way. A press conference sounds like a fine idea. I'll call a friend over at WLTX. Columbia doesn't pay near enough attention to the issues we have out here. Let's say nine in the morning. I'm sure I can make that work. Stay strong, my dear. And go on back to class now. Miss Terry will give you a note for your teacher."

Neve took the note and went to science class.

When she gave her note to Mrs. Michaels, the whole class stopped talking. Their eyes followed Neve as she walked to where her mutualism group was sitting. The distance seemed very long.

People didn't start talking again until she was in her chair.

"What happened?" Sammy said. "Everyone is saying Rose is missing. I'm sorry I didn't know about it this morning on the bus."

Something about all the students looking her way, plus all the other students pretending not to look, made Neve feel like she might cry.

"You don't have to talk about it," Aniyah said quickly.

"It's okay," Neve said. "It's just that I don't know anything. We were out running yesterday and she got ahead of me and then I couldn't find her." She couldn't mention the fog, not right then. The thought of the fog made her ill.

"Gosh, that's awful," Toni said.

"Did she have her cell phone?" Aniyah said. "Never mind, I'm sure you thought about that."

"We could ask around, call around, see if anyone has heard anything," Toni suggested.

"Good thinking!" Sammy said. And to Neve: "You could make a list of people she knows. Maybe Rose said something to somebody that could be a clue."

Neve nodded. She flipped to the back of her drawing notebook to start on what was going to be a pretty long list, and there was her *other* list. The three things Rose would do. Neve hadn't gotten to the third one yet: *Make stores put up missing-person posters!*

But class had started up again and the first group was presenting. Aniyah and Sammy were working on their group's report. Piper was across the room, pointedly *not* looking in Neve's direction. And Toni was staring at her expectantly.

Neve worked on the list of people Rose knew.

It wasn't until the end of class, after Aniyah and Toni had taken Neve's list, that Neve screwed up the nerve to say, "Um, Sammy . . . what about making missing-person posters too?"

Sammy was nodding before she finished. "Sure thing. You'll be doing the design, right?"

* * *

The principal called for a vigil for Rose during last period. Neve did not go. She spent the entire time in the girls' restroom rather than in the gymnasium; she could *not* listen to all those people talking about Rose.

Aniyah and Toni caught Neve before she stepped onto the bus but didn't mention her absence at the vigil. "We made copies of this list and we're going to make calls tonight," Aniyah said and patted Neve's shoulder.

Neve thanked them and took the seat on the bus behind Mrs. Peterson, who wore a red Dr. Who hat and insisted Neve take another peppermint. Shortly after, Sammy slid in next to her, armed with a stack of blank posters and markers from Miss Terry in the school office.

"Let's do this, let's find Rose," he said. "My mom knows a ton of businesses through her work. You've probably heard of her company, WCP Two, for 'Women Can Paint Too.' It's pretty famous."

"I haven't. But we just moved here from Columbia. Or near there."

"She goes there too, for jobs. She knows, like, everybody. We'll get these posters up all over."

During the ride, they created some simple designs: black block lettering that said MISSING GIRL above a description of Rose and what she'd been wearing.

Mrs. Peterson must've been listening in as she drove. She said, "Don't put your mama's telephone number on there. People call those numbers with such nonsense. Tell them to call the police station."

"Okay." Neve scribbled over the number she'd written and wrote instead, *Call the police station with any information at all!*

"Should we put *reward offered*?" Sammy said, poised with a marker.

"I've got fifteen dollars left over from my birthday money."

"Okay, I'm adding *reward* in. I'll give these to Mom this afternoon. And Mr. Hendriks will let me put one in the window of the grocery. You'll draw the ones that will have Rose's picture tonight?"

"Yes," Neve said. "Let me just finish this one and you can take it too."

Sammy made an outline around REWARD. "You know, I should show you my drawings sometime. Get your thoughts."

"Your mutualism cards?"

"Nah, not those. What I really like to draw is buildings," Sammy said, sketching some stars around the edges of the poster. "I'm planning on being an architect. I want to design communities, like where old people live near kids in daycares, things like that. But I want to make it a place that people can afford and that's environmentally friendly. I started out with the planning and now I'm getting into the drawing. Oh, here's my stop."

Neve blinked. She had never thought about *doing* anything with her art. And here was Sammy, planning a whole career using art. It was like Sammy was an ordinary kid with shiny hair and a shiny smile on the outside but something more unusual and interesting inside.

But then he was waving and getting off the bus.

And Rose wasn't there to talk it over with.

Neve felt sick again.

＊ ＊ ＊

Everyone besides Mrs. Peterson and Neve had left the bus when Mrs. Peterson abruptly said, "Just what do you think you're doing?"

Neve jumped. But Mrs. Peterson's eyes in the rearview mirror weren't on hers. Neve turned around to see who the driver was looking at.

The boy in the red shirt was sitting in the back row, smiling. The boy's ears seemed to have grown longer since Neve had seen him, his eyes darker, his teeth more pointed.

A prickle of fear went down Neve's spine. She was very glad, at that moment, that she sat near Mrs. Peterson.

"You have to have a note to ride home on a bus that's not yours," Mrs. Peterson said to the boy. "And I don't remember you giving me any such thing. Where'd you even come from?"

Had he been hiding below the seats? Neve wondered.

"I will depart with Neve," the boy said in a raspy voice that sounded like he had a cold. "My destination is nearby."

"No," Neve said to Mrs. Peterson. "We don't have any neighbors."

Mrs. Peterson's eyes flicked to meet Neve's, then turned back to the boy. "You can't ride a bus that's not yours with no note. I'm calling this in." She pulled into the deserted Shell station, and Neve realized they weren't far from her house.

Mrs. Peterson took her cell phone out, started punching in some numbers.

Neve slowly moved her eyes to the back of the bus.

As if he'd been waiting for her to look, the boy stood and, with that terrible grin, said, "See you soon, Neve." And he opened the emergency exit door and jumped out of the bus, the alarm blaring.

Looking out the window, Neve followed his progress. He

gave her a toothy smile from the parking lot and darted around the deserted building.

He was headed in the direction of her house.

✳ ✳ ✳

Mrs. Peterson stopped the bus at Neve's driveway. Buses from different organizations lined the street, names written on their sides: LAUREL BRANCH CHURCH. TREE OF LIFE. FOREST LAKE SENIOR LIVING. A bunch of cars too. People were milling around everywhere. Mrs. Peterson picked up her cell phone, and Neve gave her Mom's number.

"Just a courtesy call, Mrs. Fenn," Mrs. Peterson said into the phone. "As there are so many people about, you might want to pick up Neve at the street. Uh-huh. Yes, I agree." She hung up and said to Neve, "She's driving the car up here. You can explain it to her. About that boy. Didn't want to distress her, not with everything else she's got to worry about."

"Thank you." Neve said. And it wasn't long before the Volvo was there.

Once in the car, Neve told Mom about the strange boy on the bus, about how it had upset her, how it had upset Mrs. Peterson. But Mom was distracted.

"We'll tell the detective," Mom said. "But I can't imagine he'll be all that worried about a child. That sounds like a matter for the school to deal with. In any case, you are definitely *not* going outside by yourself. I'll be with you. And we are keeping the doors locked. Are you wearing Rose's cardigan?"

Neve had forgotten she'd taken it from the locker. "Yeah."

"Oh, honey," Mom said and patted Neve's knee.

Mom kept having to stop the car to talk to people. Volunteers had apparently been there all day, searching. Mom tried to meet as many as she could. Neve looked for the boy in the red shirt, but she didn't see him anywhere.

They parked and found Dad out in the yard. Neve told them about her plans.

"And Sammy is going to put up the posters," Neve said. "His mom knows a lot of businesses. Mrs. Peterson is putting one at her church. We're going to make more posters tonight. And here, I made a list of everyone Rose knows. Some of them the kids already talked to at school and they checked those off."

"Color-coded! Thank you," Mom said. "And a press conference at nine a.m. at the school? That sounds wonderful, doesn't it, Rob?"

"I'll check with Detective Rogers when he gets back, make sure the police are on board with this. I've never heard of a school doing that," Dad said.

"Principal Williams said it'd be an appeal to return Rose. From the school," Neve said.

"I don't see how it could hurt," Mom said.

The bloodhounds, the trained ones, hadn't found anything. They'd run around in circles, Dad said, which meant there was no discernible trail. To the police, it was starting to look like Rose was no longer in the area.

And Mom gave Neve the news that a dive team was coming the next day to search the lake.

"But she's a junior lifesaver," Neve said. At the YMCA, she meant. Rose had been the best in their swimming lessons, taking classes through to junior lifesaving. "She *can't* be in the lake."

"Of course not. It's just precautionary," Mom said. "Just covering all the bases."

Neve felt queasy thinking about it. Mom wouldn't let her join the search, so Neve went to her room, got out her pens and the poster paper, and began frantically working on a missing-girl poster. She sketched Rose in the pink running shorts and tank top she'd been wearing. For her hair, Neve alternated mandarin red, orange, and brown. Sky blue would have to do for Rose's eyes, though it wasn't quite right. She stared into those eyes. "Rose, where *are* you?" she whispered.

Mom later brought Neve a turkey lettuce wrap and sweet-potato chips.

"Good work. Can you bring me about a hundred more of these sandwiches?" Neve said.

"Your humor helps, it really does," Mom said. "Why don't I get you some of the oatmeal cookies too? They're delicious."

"Sure, Mom."

They were both pretending. Neve's stomach was churning too much for her to feel like eating, and Mom had purple circles under her eyes. Neve doubted she'd eaten much of anything either.

Please, Neve thought, *let all this work.* Let the things she had started that day work.

But by eight that night, it was clear that nothing was working.

Dad had talked to Detective Rogers, and he'd insisted on canceling the school's press conference. The police chief would do one from the station when they were ready. The detective said the public got desensitized and confused if too much information was put out from too many sources. He also said all the untrained searchers, despite their good intentions, were contaminating the search area, and the police were trying to discourage them from coming out. What's more, the police had already posted missing-person notices downtown. They didn't need kids creating hand-drawn posters.

Everything Neve had done at school that day had been a complete waste of time.

She took her notebook out of her backpack. "A new list," she said. "I need a new list." But when she flipped to the back of the book to start it, she gasped.

A detailed pencil drawing of a knife. The handle was unusual—it looked like a deer hoof, complete with dewclaws and little pencil marks indicating the fur. The blade itself looked deadly, coming to a sharp point. She reached out to rip the page from her notebook but found she didn't want to touch it.

She certainly had not drawn it. And it hadn't been in her notebook when she was in science class. Had someone sneaked into her bedroom and drawn it? But the backpack had been at her feet for hours. And Mom had been in the family room talking almost nonstop, either on her phone or to people coming to the door. No one could have gotten past her. And Neve would have seen anyone who had.

When had the backpack been out of her sight? The only time was the last period of the day. The vigil for Rose. Neve had left the backpack in the keyboarding classroom and pretended she was going to the vigil when in fact she'd gone to the restroom and hadn't come out again until it was time to go to the buses.

The alarming truth seemed to be this: someone had drawn the knife *in her notebook* while the entire school was in the gymnasium talking about Rose. Who could have done that? Who *would* have done that? And why?

That boy. That strange boy who'd been on the bus. Who had stared at her in school.

Neve forced herself to rip the drawing out of the notebook. "Mom, you need to see this," she said, walking into the family room.

Mom was snoring, sound asleep on the divan, fallen over at an odd angle. She looked so fragile right then, like the slightest touch would break her in half.

The detective. That was who needed to see this, really. Neve didn't know what the boy had to do with the fog, but maybe she had it all wrong. Maybe the boy knew something. She folded the drawing and put it in her pocket.

She went back into her bedroom, piled pillows on her bed, and put the quilt over them to make it look like she was underneath. Mom was so tired, that might actually work. Then Neve fished in her closet for her flashlight, found it, and changed out of the cardigan into a black hooded sweatshirt. Before sneaking out, she stared out the bedroom window. The flashlights of the searchers bobbed in the darkness.

She pressed her nose against the window and blinked her lashes against the cold glass.

If only yesterday afternoon had gone differently. If only she'd run faster, had been right beside Rose when the fog came. They could have fought it together. Or maybe they could have held hands and outrun it. Or maybe Neve could have gone with Rose to wherever she had ended up.

It would be better than being here without her.

So much time had passed since Rose disappeared.

Where *was* she?

Chapter Eleven

ROSE WAS IN A BOX.

She tried pressing her fingers to her forehead, pinching the top of her nose, and squeezing the skin between her thumb and forefinger. She had tested out crouching, curling up in a fetal position, and making herself into a V, and she was currently attempting to lie on her back with her knees up. The plywood box was no bigger than three feet square, a most uncomfortable size.

Nothing she did lessened the pain that roared behind her eyes.

She tried to avoid triggering events, but once a migraine came on, the only thing to do was lie down. She'd put a pillow under her knees, a cool washcloth on her forehead, and earplugs in her ears and demand to be left alone in complete quiet and complete dark. She'd sleep the pain away.

Well, she had the complete quiet and the complete dark. She did not, however, have the pillow, the washcloth, or the earplugs. And she definitely did not have the sleep.

The vomit in the box didn't help. Maybe she'd been sick

because of the dizzying ride with the fog. Or maybe it was because she'd refused to give the dreadful Mrs. Katch—or so she'd introduced herself—the satisfaction of hearing screams or crying and had instead done a lot of silent raging. The raging hadn't made Rose feel better; it had made her more nauseated.

She hugged her water bottle to her chest. It was empty. She'd drunk the last of the water hours ago. But it was the only thing she had besides her single shoe, which she was using as a pillow.

It struck her then, as she was shifting positions for maybe the hundredth time, that the box she was in was about the size of the ones Neve was always constructing.

Neve felt safe in the boxes, or so she said. They made her feel calm. And the times she talked Rose into going inside one, Rose had felt safe too. Not because of the box—which made her feel claustrophobic—but because of Neve being there.

Like that time under the beach towel. Rose had been four, Neve three. They'd just come off the water slide at the public pool when Rose realized she didn't see the babysitter anywhere. She'd gone into a spinning panic, running in circles around Neve, who climbed into a chair, water wings and all, and put a beach towel over her head like a tent. Neve patted the seat next to her, and once Rose calmed down a little, she climbed up and let Neve put the beach towel over her head too. "She'll be back," Neve said. And Rose replied, "You talked!" Because Neve hadn't before and the adults were really upset about it. Neve just smiled with those tiny baby teeth as if she'd known how to talk the whole time. She had just been waiting for something that truly needed to be said.

Rose stared up into the darkness, her back pressed to the hard floor of the box, her bent knees digging into the plywood, and thought about what it would be like if Neve were here instead.

Well, for sure Neve would *not* have yelled silently into the box, sucking up all the oxygen and making herself panic even more. She also wouldn't have thrashed around so much or pushed against the sides of the box or clawed out a loose nail, getting splinters in her fingers.

No, Neve would have carefully touched the sides of the box, the door hinges, the air holes, and noted that there were no other openings anywhere. She would have run her fingers across the dozens of nails and realized that extracting a single nail wasn't going to loosen the sides of the box.

Then Neve would have been still. She would have stayed calm. Maybe she would even have threaded her fingers together over her stomach.

Next, Neve would have looked up into the dark with that cool mossy-green stare. She would have taken deep breaths—in through the nose, out through the mouth. And once her pulse slowed and her panic subsided, she would have used her brain, in pain or not.

Neve would have gone over what she had to work with.

A metal water bottle, stainless steel. Not tough enough to break the door down. A shoe, rubber sole and laces. A tank and shorts. Sports bra, underwear. A hair tie. It wasn't a very impressive list.

Then there was the box.

Plywood, it felt like. Too bad Rose wasn't a martial artist. Maybe she could have broken it with her bare hands (she'd tried, dozens of times).

Nails. It'd taken hours to extract the one. And most had been nailed from the outside anyway.

Hinges. What did she know about those? At the old house, she remembered, Dad had taken the laundry-room door off the hinges to fit the new dryer inside. Rose had watched him do it.

Now, *that* could be helpful. Her heart beat faster and she sat up slowly, breathing carefully. *Don't get yourself worked up.* Mom's voice in her head.

Rose had no inkling of the time. She'd been in the box for many hours. Days, maybe. She was so far past hunger, she wasn't hungry anymore, only thirsty. But no, it couldn't have been *too* many days, because she hadn't died of dehydration. And there had been only one time when she'd heard a bird chirping and guessed it might be morning. So maybe only one day?

No noises from outside the box. Mrs. Katch had a habit of talking to herself, but Rose hadn't heard her for some time.

She felt for the nail. The one measly nail. She'd been lying on it. *There you are*, she thought. *You precious thing.*

She set the nail on the bottom of the hinge like she'd seen Dad do. Then, with the water bottle, she tapped ever so lightly. Listened for what must've been a full minute. Then set to it harder. It took three good taps to remove the first pin. A few more for the second.

The chain and padlock clinked as she swung the door off

its hinges. The kitchen was lit only by the moonlight coming in through the window.

She took in a breath of nighttime air, but it came with a vile smell. She kept her eyes away from the smell's source, the something horrible she'd glimpsed on her way in. The something that sat silently. The something that would no doubt look even more horrifying now, in the dead of night.

A rotting corpse. Probably one of Mrs. Katch's victims. *Why did she keep it in the house?*

Rose focused only on escaping.

The bottom half of the Dutch door was jammed shut, but the top opened.

She climbed out into the dark.

Chapter Twelve

THE WIND BLEW through the trees over Neve's head, whispered in the long grass, murmured in the silver moonlight: *She's not here.*

"Then where?" Neve said aloud, shining her flashlight on a fallen log.

She was talking to herself. She was across the road from her house, in the woods, staying well away from the other searchers, the sweatshirt's hood firmly over her head. The closest flashlight beam was fifty feet away. She'd found an officer, given her the drawing of the knife, and extracted a promise from her to give it to the detective. But now Neve didn't want to be seen. If she ran into Dad, she'd be sent back to the house.

She closed her eyes and listened to the sounds of the night. As if she might hear Rose calling from wherever she was if she concentrated hard enough.

Like that time years ago. Mom loved to tell the story: Neve had the flu and was supposed to be resting. But instead, she came stumbling into the kitchen, insisting Rose was in pain and that Mom needed to do something. Mom called over to the Smiths' house, where Rose was playing, and learned that Rose had done a cartwheel off the porch and, it turned out, had fractured her arm. Neve couldn't explain how she'd known, if she'd felt it or seen it or heard Rose calling.

Neve listened now.

All she heard was the wind, an owl, hooting over and over, and a lone cricket too stubborn to call it a summer. No Rose.

Neve opened her eyes.

No hound either. She would have liked his company in the dark. But after she fed him earlier, he'd pricked up his ears and run off up the driveway. Some help he was.

Behind the log, moss glowed eerily. Neve swept the flashlight beam up and away.

And lit up a face. A face she hadn't wanted to see.

The boy in the red shirt. Smiling. Not ten feet away.

Neve sucked in a breath. Her heart pounded. "Why are you here? Are you following me?" She kept the beam of light pointed in his face as if she could pin him there, keep him from coming closer.

He didn't seem bothered by the light. He didn't shield his eyes. Those oddly dark eyes. He wasn't even as tall as she was, she noticed. It wasn't particularly reassuring. "The soul of the fox has been stolen," he said in that raspy voice. "And now the child. It is the pattern."

"A child . . . are you talking about Rose? Are you looking for her too? What pattern?"

He tilted his head to the side as if confused by what she was saying. "Why do you not search the swamp? Swamps have a way of hiding things."

The swamp? "I thought that was far away in the woods. Were you at the swamp? Did you see Rose?" Neve was not going to search a swamp while the boy was nearby. He seemed just the sort to push her in.

"You must go to the swamp. You must find the knife. And you must kill her with it."

The air on Neve's cheeks was cold. She backed up a step. Clearly, he'd been the one who'd left the drawing. "Kill . . . Rose?"

"Not Rose. The one who has taken her. And it must be you. You must slide it between her ribs, into the heart."

An awful deed to imagine. "Me? Why? Do you know who took her?"

"The road is in plain sight, but only a child can see it. It is an ordinary road, but only a child can walk it."

"You're not making sense. You're scaring me."

The boy just kept smiling. And the more he smiled, the more he looked like he was wearing a mask that was melting away. As if underneath, his skin was no longer young, his ears were much bigger, and his teeth were long and pointed. His eyes seemed to get darker while she watched.

Neve suddenly had an odd notion: this was no boy.

She turned and ran.

Chapter Thirteen

ROSE DIDN'T GET FAR.

The fog was waiting for her outside of Mrs. Katch's house, lurking there.

Before Rose had taken many steps, before she'd gotten her bearings, before she could even curse it properly, the fog had swept her up, carried her back to the kitchen, and tossed her into the box *for the second time.*

A hailstorm of nails. The points stuck through the door. No hinges on this one.

Rose groaned, slumping against the plywood, missing her water bottle and her shoe, both lost on the grounds somewhere. Her ankle throbbed. She'd twisted it somehow. Her forehead hurt too. She'd bumped it.

The door was shut but good. She was never, ever getting out of this box, was never going to see her family again.

"She'll be back." A small, reedy voice.

Rose flinched.

It was Neve. Her bony shoulder pressed up against Rose's, sticky with sunscreen and smelling of chlorine, those water wings dripping. The beach towel was rough and warm on Rose's head; trickles of sunlight came through, shining on Neve's white eyelashes and turning her eyes as green as a cat's.

"I'm hallucinating," Rose said. She was not four years old at the public pool, scared because she couldn't find her babysitter. She was there in the plywood box. She knew she was. She felt the wood below her. It had developed new splinters while she was gone, and she was going to die there, hallucinating, with a butt full of splinters. And she was likely seeing her life flash before her eyes, as she'd heard happened right before you died, and soon she'd be as mushy and rotten as the corpse sitting in the kitchen.

"She'll be back," imaginary Neve said again. That three-year-old's voice was surprisingly clear considering she wasn't really there.

"Why do you keep saying that?" Rose said.

And Neve's gaze was firm and steady like it'd been thousands of times before, all those times Rose was upset about this thing or that, because Neve always had a reason why everything was going to be fine, and that was when Rose realized what the voice was trying to tell her.

Oh, Rose thought, and imaginary Neve disappeared. The vision had seemed so real, so *sure*. Rose decided to believe it.

The woman, Mrs. Katch, would be back. She hadn't captured Rose for the sole purpose of putting her in a box to die. The woman had brought Rose there for a reason. And the reason would be outside the box. That meant there would be another chance for action. Another chance for an escape.

Rose's breathing slowed.

Yes. Back to making a plan.

She had nothing more to work with in the box. But what was *outside* the box? What had she seen, glimpsed, on her way into and out of this tiny prison, between her and the fog that waited outside? What was there besides the horrible Mrs. Katch?

A kitchen. A corpse. A knife.

Ah, Rose thought.

A knife made out of a deer hoof. Mrs. Katch was always chopping or slicing with it. Rose had seen it, heard it. And it'd been lying on the stove, glinting in the moonlight, when she attempted her escape. She doubted it would work against the fog. But maybe, just maybe, it would work against Mrs. Katch.

That's right. What I'm going to do, Rose thought as she slowly breathed in and out, *is get that knife.*

Chapter Fourteen

NEVE DREAMED of a bloodred moon in a black sky. It glared at her all night long.

And in the morning, in the kitchen, while she searched for some breakfast, she could still see the moon behind her lids, imprinted there like an afterimage from a camera's flash.

The evening before seemed like a dream too. Had she really found a drawing of a knife in her notebook? Had she really talked to the boy in the red shirt? It felt unreal. All the talk of swamps and stabbing people. The frightening way the boy looked. When Neve got back to the house, Mom had been in the same position, still snoring. Neve was starting to think she'd created the entire outing in her head.

Sticking out of Mom's purse on the kitchen table was a large manila envelope, folded to fit inside. On the front: *Mrs. Lilliana Fenn. Urgent. Hand Deliver to Addressee Only.*

Neve shouldn't look inside the envelope. She knew she shouldn't, as it was not her envelope. But the frustration from the night before was still strong. The feeling of not being able to do anything. Of not *knowing* anything.

Before she'd much thought about it, the envelope was in her hands. The tape was ripped, the paper torn. The envelope had already been opened. Maybe that made Neve's offense less severe.

Inside was a sheaf of paper. Official logos. Lawyer words she didn't understand. But there was something that stood out.

Robert David Fenn requests primary physical custody of the minor child Rose Alessia Fenn.

It wasn't so much what was there but what wasn't.

A yellow sticky note from Mom's lawyer: *Did you know he was going to try this?*

Neve suddenly needed to sit on the floor. Everything down there smelled faintly of bleach. The paint on the kitchen cabinets was chipped, she noticed, particularly around the edges. The papers in her lap poked her thighs, but she couldn't summon the energy to move them away.

She didn't know what she'd expected. Some official investigative news about Rose. Some information Mom hadn't told her, like maybe she'd asked Dad for a million dollars. Shocking love letters from Mom's secret new boyfriend, even. But Neve hadn't expected this. Dad's *recent action*.

Though it made perfect sense, she knew.

Neve's chest *thunk-thunk*ed. A clawing in there. The secret, demanding to be thought about. She didn't want to think about it. But the secret didn't care what she wanted. It replayed in her head.

The night before Mom started packing, Neve had been heading downstairs for a glass of water when she heard her parents talking. Something about the tone of the conversation had stopped Neve dead on the steps. What she heard was this:

Mom: "You know why."

Dad: "I really don't. Your life here is great. I bend over backwards to make your life great."

Mom: "I'm not talking about my life. Your attitude hasn't improved. I told you I won't stand for it anymore. You have two wonderful girls. *Two.* I've had it with you acting like Neve is somehow *substandard*."

There was more. Neve continued to listen. But she'd gotten the point. Mom was sick of Dad being obvious about who his favorite daughter was, and therefore Mom was leaving and taking both girls with her. It was apparently a conversation they'd had before. Dad kept denying there was an issue, saying Mom was being ridiculous.

The part about Rose being Dad's favorite was no surprise to Neve. She'd known since a Christmas morning when she was very small. Dad had videoed Rose opening her presents, but when Neve started opening hers, Dad got up to make waffles. Mom took over the videoing, and Rose did a lot of oohing and aahing over Neve's unwrapping (protecting her even then, Neve realized later), but Neve understood: whatever Rose did was more interesting and important.

Dad's little comments over the years made it even more obvious. When Mom said Neve couldn't eat something because of her wheat allergy, he'd say, "Here we go again." When Mom claimed Neve was artistic, he'd say her boxes were "a strange way for her to spend her time." When Mom said Neve had a great sense of humor, he'd say, "She does?"

No, the favorite-daughter part was no surprise. A hard little knot of pain had been in Neve's heart since that Christmas morning. The Mom-leaving-him-because-of-it part, well, that *had* been a surprise. And the hard little knot had burst open into the full-blown secret. She'd staggered to bed that night without saying a word to anyone.

But now this. Dad's *recent action.*

Neve might have been stuck to the kitchen floor. She just sat there, feeling the *thunk-thunk* of her heart in her chest. Feeling the *thunk-thunk* of that pain.

Dad shuffled into the kitchen, headed for the coffeepot. He wore a white undershirt, wrinkled khaki pants, and his glasses. His hair stuck up more than yesterday. He almost stepped on Neve before he noticed her. "What are you doing on the floor?"

Neve's pain came out as anger. "Why would you take her away from me?"

Dad started. His gaze went to the papers in her lap. "Those are Mom's papers."

"It's not as if I wouldn't know eventually. Why would you do it?"

"I'm not doing anything. It's what Rose wants."

"I don't believe you." Neve and Rose did not leave each other. They did not.

"I don't have time for this. I need to get to the sink. I need to refill the coffeepot."

"I won't move out of the way until you tell me."

He snorted. "Tell you what?"

"Tell me why you'd do this."

"Rose wants to go to the tennis academy in Spartanburg. It's over two hours away from here. It's a day program. She got in, but she can't live here and go. Don't you know all that?"

Two hours away? In another part of the state? Alarm bells rang in Neve's head. "*You* want her to go, I bet. You want her to live with you. It's not Rose. It's you."

"It's not my idea. Rose wants to be better at tennis. The academy would help her do that. You could go too if you wanted to up your game. Get your ranking back up. I'm sure you'd get in. Could be good for you. *Now* can I get coffee?"

A sliver of doubt crept into Neve's heart. She let him get by. It sounded like the truth. All Rose's talk of tennis, her threatening to move in with Dad . . . had Rose been trying to tell her? Neve felt sick, nauseated.

Mom walked in wearing a bathrobe. "Why are you both talking so loudly?"

Dad said, "Neve's been reading your mail."

Mom looked at the papers in Neve's lap. "Honey, that's not for you to worry about. That's just lawyer stuff. Maneuvering. And none of it's important right now. Let's find Rose first. All of that will sort itself out."

"Yes, let's keep our eyes on the prize," Dad said.

Dad's prize. Neve started to shake. Now, on top of Rose being missing, stolen by a horrible fog, Dad was hovering like a vulture, waiting to snatch Rose away as soon as she reappeared.

"Neve, honey, that's not going to happen," Mom said as if she could read Neve's mind. "My attorney says that's not going to happen. Come here."

Neve was shaking so hard, her teeth chattered. "I'm not coming there." She got unsteadily to her feet and took a step toward the pantry. She needed to get food for the dog.

"I'm just trying to accommodate what people ask me to do." Dad turned on the faucet. His back was to them. "It's a lot of trouble for me. Moving to Spartanburg. It's not like it's easy for me to do. I have a job. I don't even know if they'll approve my transfer."

"It will all work out." Mom's eyes were on Neve. "I'll make sure it does. Nothing is going to happen that's not the best solution for everyone involved."

Mom had not been surprised by this. She had already read the papers. Neve's anger was now directed at Mom too. "You knew about it. You told the detective."

"I just wanted him to have all the information."

"It wasted police resources," Dad said. "They sent people over to the other house. They talked to the neighbors. All those resources could have been used here. They could have already found her."

"Don't get yourself worked up," Mom said.

"I'm not worked up!" Dad said. "I'm just trying to get my coffee, and everyone is giving me a hard time. I'm not getting any sleep on that hideous blue thing that passes for a couch."

"It's a divan," Mom said. "And it's teal." She raised her chin in a way Neve wasn't used to.

"You knew about the tennis school, about Rose wanting to go," Neve said to Mom.

"I knew," Mom said. "Rose wasn't ready to tell you yet, though, or talk to me about it. I was respecting her wishes."

"I don't believe you," Neve said. "Rose and I need to be together. You know that."

"I'm not sure I do know that, honey. But now's not the time," Mom said.

"I'm going out. To look for Rose. It's been too long. We should have found her by now."

"No," Mom said. "The divers are coming to search the lake today. This is not the place for a child."

"They think there might be gators. This is some kind of place your mom brought you to, eh?" Dad said.

Something squeezed Neve's insides. "Alligators?" She could barely get the word out. She hadn't seen any alligators here, but could there be?

"Stop it," Mom said to Dad. "There are *not* any alligators this far north. And the detective did not say that. You being alarmist again is *not* helping."

Dad slammed his coffee cup on the counter. "*Gators* are alarming."

"I need to be here," Neve said. "*Especially* if you're looking in the lake, I need to be here."

"I'm sorry," Mom said. "But you're going to school and that's final. I'll call the school the instant I know anything."

Neve was so furious she couldn't speak. She yanked a box of rice cereal out of the pantry. The hound could eat the whole box as far as she was concerned. He could eat every last thing out of their pantry. She marched to the back door, opened it.

The hound was there. He had something in his mouth. Bright orange with a yellow lace, double knotted. You couldn't miss those colors.

Rose's other shoe.

Chapter Fifteen

"YOU FOUND HER!" Neve said to the hound.

The hound dropped Rose's running shoe into Neve's hands. The cereal box she'd been carrying fell to the ground, forgotten. She hugged the shoe to her chest. "Where is she? Is she okay? Not the lake, right? I'm sure it's not the lake."

His tail wagged. He sniffed the cereal box on the ground.

She put out a hand to close the door behind her. Too late. Mom and Dad were already there. "What is it? Who's there?" they said.

"It's nothing," Neve said, trying to hide the shoe from their sight.

"What's that you have there?" Mom said. "My God, Neve. Is that what I think it is?"

"I don't know. I'm not sure," Neve said.

But Mom and Dad were already removing the running shoe from her hands.

"Rob, it's the other shoe. Of the pair Rose was wearing," Mom said.

"Call the detective," Dad said. "Let me get this dog."

"You don't need to get him," Neve said. "He can lead us to where he found it."

"Here, dog. Good dog." Dad moved toward the hound, arms out.

The hound backed away. His tail had stopped wagging.

"You're scaring him," Neve said. "Don't grab him."

"Come here, dog. Be a good dog," Dad said.

The hound ducked out of Dad's grasp.

"He doesn't want you to grab him," Neve said.

"Try bending down," Mom said. "Waiting for him to come to you."

"You do the waiting," Dad said. "I'm. Getting. This. Dog." He lunged for the hound.

The hound gave a short bark, rotating on his back legs, gracefully avoiding Dad.

"Leave him alone," Neve said.

"Look at me, dog, I'm being serious here," Dad said.

"Honestly, Rob," Mom said. She had her cell phone out.

Dad chased the hound out into the yard, Neve running after them. The hound was much faster than them both. His panting looked like a smile. It was possible he thought it was a game. But eventually he tired of it and disappeared into the trees.

"Now he won't be able to help us!" Neve said. She had scrapes up her legs. She was still wearing pajamas. Her feet were covered in dirt and mud.

"You don't know anything about it," Dad said.

"I do so—you chased him away!"

"Stop it, you two," Mom shouted from the back door.

Dad's glasses were crooked. He glared at Neve.

Neve glared back. The pain was *thunk-thunk*ing. "I know what you're thinking," she said. He wished it were her, she knew. He wished it were her that was missing and not Rose.

"That everything's gone to hell?" Dad said. "That I don't know how to fix it? That I'm desperate enough to chase a mangy old dog for leads?"

"Well, no," Neve said. She hadn't known he was thinking all that. She couldn't remember ever actually *asking* Dad what he thought about anything. Rose had always been there to deal with Dad. They didn't do so much talking, Neve and Dad.

He took off his glasses and rubbed his nose. "Look, I don't know what to do with you lately. I know you're worried about your sister. We're worried too. But we have to work together here and not be at each other's throats."

Neve frowned at him. He did look worried. He also might have some new gray hairs at his temples. The chunk of pain in her chest shifted, just slightly. They both loved Rose, that was for certain.

"The detective is on the phone," Mom called out to them. "Rob, he wants to talk to you."

Dad ran to the phone. He was out of breath as he listened. "Yes, get them out here," he said. When he hung up, he told Mom, "They're bringing in another group of dogs. This group is from Lugoff. Their dogs are older. Maybe these will be better trained."

"This is the first good news we've had since she went missing," Mom said. The three of them stepped inside and she put the shoe into a plastic baggie.

"It's because of the dog. You owe him," Neve said. She looked out the window into the backyard while she wiped her feet on the mat. The hound hadn't come back.

"Yes, you're right," Mom said. "We owe him a lot. Do you know what this means?"

"That you ruined the best chance I had of finding Rose?"

"No, honey, think about it. The police have looked on the street, all around where you girls were. That area was *scoured*. This shoe was *not* there. The dog finding it could mean she's still in the area. Even if a vehicle picked her up, it didn't take her far."

"I told you it wasn't some vehicle. It was the fog," Neve said.

Mom ignored this. She looked at the shoe in the plastic bag as if it were a miracle. "Just think of the clues on this shoe. Like the type of soil, pollen, seeds around where she walked."

"You're a dirt expert now, I guess," Neve said, though she was beginning to come around to the possibilities.

"What I *do* know is that that dog of yours has given us some new hope."

✳ ✳ ✳

On the bus that morning, Sammy sat next to Neve, who was in the seat behind Mrs. Peterson. "We need to make more posters," he said. "The ones we put up yesterday got taken down. The grocer said he had to."

"Do you believe in magic?" Neve said.

"What? Why? Did someone say I did?" His smile was extra-big. He was unexpectedly defensive. So maybe he *did* believe in magic.

Neve looked out the window. They were driving through the small downtown area. "Piper believes in magic. She thinks it was something magic that took her sister."

"What do you think? Do you think magic took Rose?" He still wore that Sammy smile. Neve wasn't looking at him but she could feel it. And she couldn't tell if that meant he thought what she was saying was strange. Mary Ann McDonald in fifth grade had been like that, smiling all the time. Neve thought it meant that the girl liked her, liked what Neve was saying, but it turned out that what Mary Ann liked was having material to use the next time she made fun of Neve behind her back.

"I don't know what to think," Neve said. "I was watching and she disappeared. How could that happen?" She didn't tell him about the fog. She didn't think she could take one more person not believing about the fog. "And I keep dreaming about . . . strange things."

"My mom says dreams can tell us a lot about ourselves," Sammy said.

"Like maybe I'm strange?" Neve said, and her face heated.

"No, no, that's not what I meant," Sammy said. "I mean you could be trying to tell yourself something. Like your unconscious self knows something your conscious self hasn't realized yet. I've realized stuff because my mom studies trees."

"What?" Neve said. She wasn't sure what trees had to do with dreams. Or with Rose. And didn't his mom have a business? "For her painting?"

"Hang on," Sammy said. "That's not what I wanted to say either. She does it in her spare time. And since it's just the two of us, me and my mom, I used to have to go with her on the weekends while she did her research. For *years*. PhDs take a long time even if you don't also have a business to run. Woods, creeks, swamps. I went everywhere looking at those trees. And I saw all sorts of things. A fungus that turns ants into zombie slaves, and these anole lizards that change color in, like, a second, and a couple of times we heard a crying woman Mom said was a bob-cat except it did *not* sound like a bobcat. Really, you would not believe all the stuff out there. It's right in front of us sometimes. The world is stranger than we think."

Mrs. Peterson—wearing a hat that made it look like she had eyes in the back of her head—said, "Amen to that."

They were pulling up to the school.

"I should have told Mom about the boy," Neve said. "Should've told Dad too. Even if it might've been a dream, even if I would've gotten in trouble for sneaking out, I should have told them."

"What boy?" Sammy said.

"He's here in the school, or at least he was. He was at my house last night. He drew a knife in my notebook."

Sammy's mouth fell open. "He did *what?*"

"I'll show him to you," Neve said.

"You're talking about the boy who was on the bus without a note?" Mrs. Peterson said. "Tell Principal Williams about that. Call me if you need to. Bus office did not know who that was."

"Okay," Neve said.

And that was what she intended to do when she went to the principal's office.

She just got distracted by the press conference.

＊ ＊ ＊

Two men were already in Principal Williams's office when Miss Terry waved Neve in. One had a navy jacket and a shaved head and the other had a salt-and-pepper beard and a large camera.

"Um, hello?" Neve said.

"Good, you're here," Principal Williams said.

"I thought the press conference was canceled," Neve said in a small voice.

"This is more of an interview," the principal said. "Mr. Chen there is a personal friend of mine. He understands the need for more coverage. Despite what that *detective* may say about it."

The man with the shaved head, Mr. Chen, said, "We'll talk about your sister. About how much you miss her. How much you want her returned. Easy-peasy. These interviews are great for getting the public more involved and aware." The cameraman was adjusting the lens.

Principal Williams was applying lipstick. "I'll talk about what a wonderful student Rose is. How everyone here already loves her. Your family can show the photo."

"The photo?" Neve squeaked.

"Are your parents bringing it?" the principal said. "We haven't had school photos yet. We don't have one of her here."

"We can run the same one we've been using," Mr. Chen said. "It's no biggie."

"Um," Neve said. "Maybe we should call them?"

"Are they running late?" the principal said. "Didn't they get my e-mail?"

"I've got a few extra minutes," Mr. Chen said. "But not a ton of time."

"I told them about the press conference, but Dad said the detective canceled it. I don't think they checked e-mail," Neve said. "I think they're at home."

"You mean . . . they're not coming?" the principal said.

"No can do without the parents," Mr. Chen said. "She's a minor."

"Oh dear," the principal said. "Can we do it with just me?"

"We can film it. Not sure they'll run it without the family. Here goes nothing, then."

Neve felt short of breath. Why hadn't she insisted Mom and Dad come to the school? Couldn't she have done *something* to keep the interview from being ruined?

"Are you all right, Neve?" the principal said. "Would you like a glass of water? Let me call the counselor in for you."

"No, thank you," Neve said, though she did feel shaky. She left the office, went out into the hall. Miss Terry didn't stop her. When Aniyah came up and said they hadn't had any luck with the people they'd called, that maybe Neve needed to make a new list, she could barely nod, could barely grasp what Aniyah said.

Rose was depending on Neve. But all Neve did was mess up one thing after another.

* * *

Neve saw the tomato hat before she saw the girl.

Piper was at her locker.

What an interesting thing, Neve thought. To put on a tomato hat just because you felt like it. For some reason, it made her think of that plaid shirt she'd had in fourth grade. The one everyone had made fun of. A pieced-together monstrosity of different plaid patterns, huge on her because it had once belonged to Grandpa. She had loved that shirt so much. She wondered what had happened to it.

"I'm sorry, Piper," Neve said. "About not believing you. I'm . . . something happened last night. And Sammy said . . . well, I think I believe you now. I hope you'll still talk to me."

Piper stared at her for a long moment. "Are you okay?"

"Yes. No. I just screwed up a TV interview."

"Why are you doing TV interviews?"

"I was just thinking that's what Rose would do."

"Why are you doing what Rose would do? It's not like she's

any better than you or would know any more than you about this."

Any plan of action Neve ever considered, she ran past Rose first. Neve was more of the suggester, Rose the decider. As to who was better . . . Neve shrugged.

"If you want my opinion, it's time to start listening to your gut. Thinking about what *you* would do and doing it," Piper said.

"I'm not sure what I would do," Neve said.

"Well, you're an artist. Artists are the observers of the world. You can start by observing my research. In the library. At lunch."

"You discovered something new?"

"Four years ago, on the day the Bethune girl went missing, fog was reported."

"It was?"

"Yes, and the other times too, according to the National Weather Service library in Columbia. I'll tell you all about it," Piper said. "Oh, and here, take a tomato. It's a vegetable that's really a fruit, you know. It'll make you feel better."

Chapter Sixteen

IT DIDN'T HAPPEN the way Rose planned.

When the door of the box finally opened, when Rose actually had the chance to do something — make a break for it or grab the knife — her eyes were blinded in the sudden light, her limbs were stiff from being cramped up for so long, and she was weak from not having eaten anything. What's more, she'd been asleep when the door opened, and by the time she was fully awake, she found herself tied to a heavy wooden chair with Mrs. Katch studying her.

Mrs. Katch with her perfect gray curls, perfect skin, and perfectly blank expression, her eyes blue as ice. She wasn't right, this Mrs. Katch. And not just because she was a kidnapper.

"Today's the day!" Mrs. Katch said.

Rose flinched. Her chair was at the kitchen table, she realized. She was being forced to sit at the table. She couldn't help glancing to her left at what sat next to her. The corpse. Rose had glimpsed it and smelled it before, but now she could see it. It wore a navy blue suit, pearl jewelry, and a hat with a feather. It had once been a woman. Maybe the woman had died sitting right there at the table. The sight was gruesome. Rose quickly looked away. "Dinner that bad?" Rose said. Her voice came out like a croak; her lips were dry and cracked.

Mrs. Katch laughed. Rose found she didn't like the laugh. The blank expression was much better. When she was finished, Mrs. Katch said, "Amusing. I can see why you're so favored, back where you come from." She pushed a bowl in front of her.

Water.

Rose drank from the bowl like a dog. Some of the water went into her nose, and she coughed for some time. When she'd finally gotten her breath, she said, "Why?" *Why was she here?* she meant. She just couldn't get the rest out.

Black dress to her ankles, buttons down the front, and a lace collar — Mrs. Katch dressed like her clothes came from a hundred-year-old closet. Or like she was on her way to a Goth convention. But she didn't leave this place. Not in the way normal people left. Rose knew that too. The ride with the fog had clued her in. This place was anything but ordinary.

"It's not personal," Mrs. Katch said. "But the blood moon doesn't appear that often. And the requirements of the spell are very specific. Very hard to fulfill. I've got a midnight deadline." She picked up a pair of hunting pliers, knobby and stained. "Voilà."

Rose shrank back.

"Relax," Mrs. Katch said. "For now, I just need a tooth."

Chapter Seventeen

"**Ow!**" **Neve said,** clapping a hand to her cheek. Her eyes watered, it hurt so much. It was as if someone had yanked a tooth right out of her mouth. But all her teeth were accounted for. Maybe it was a cavity or a stress reaction, or maybe she was feeling . . . "Rose?"

She felt him looking then. From the end of the school hallway. The boy in the red shirt.

His eyes in shadow, covered by his hair. Watching her. Smiling.

His shirt wasn't quite right for middle school, Neve realized. A solid red button-up, but it was long, like a tunic. He also wore tall black boots over black pants. And he carried nothing. No notebook. No backpack. Nothing.

What kind of student wore clothes like that and had no books?

She remembered her frightening thought from the night before—that he *wasn't* a boy, not really. "I want to talk to you!" she said. She ran toward him, only to be stopped almost immediately by Mrs. Michaels, the hall monitor.

"No running. And choose lunchroom or library," Mrs. Michaels said as the warning bell rang. But she added a sympathetic smile to show she wasn't angry.

It didn't matter. The boy was gone.

✳ ✳ ✳

Neve and Piper were the only ones in the library. Even the librarian was gone; she had left to microwave her lunch.

"He was there again. I saw that boy just now in the hall," Neve said. "And I felt . . . actually, I'm not sure what I felt."

"Have some salad. It's dairy-free mozzarella," Piper said. Grape tomatoes toothpicked with bits of the imitation cheese, some dressing drizzled over. She and Pops had made them, she said.

Neve took a toothpick of salad. It was delicious. "He was at my house last night, or at least I think he was. He told me . . ." He'd told her she had to kill someone. She hoped she *had* imagined that.

Piper lugged a thick South Carolina atlas over from the shelves and opened it to a page of maps. "Here we go," she said. "What'd he tell you?"

"I'll tell you after we look at this. What *am* I looking at?"

"All these blue pockets are bodies of water around Etters." Piper pointed with her pencil.

Neve didn't understand why that was significant. "Okay . . ."

"Well, what is fog?" Piper sounded like a teacher.

Neve was tired and her tooth ached. She helped herself to another toothpick of salad. "Just go ahead and tell me."

"Water droplets!" Piper said as if she'd discovered something amazing. "Like a cloud. Except, according to our good friend *Merriam-Webster,* fog is different from a cloud because it's found in the lower atmosphere, near the ground. It's formed more locally, from a nearby body of water or from moist ground or marshes. Thus . . ." She tapped the page again.

"But if it's magic, maybe it doesn't need water."

"It's still fog. We have to start somewhere."

"There's so many of them."

"We could go one by one. Process of elimination." Piper was starting to look less cheery.

There were a *lot* of blue places on the page. But Neve didn't want to sound discouraging. "Okay. Where do you think we should start?"

"Being positive, like your shirt?"

Neve glanced down, saw AVOID NEGATIVITY $F(x)=|x|$. It was one of several math T-shirts Mom had given her. Neve had just grabbed it out of the drawer that morning. "Rose hates this shirt," she said. She hadn't remembered to put on any makeup these past two days; Rose would hate that too.

Sammy came in. "I heard you two were in here. Are you making posters?"

"We're working on something different now," Neve said.

"You are? Can I help?"

"No," Piper said at the same time Neve said, "Yes."

Neve glanced at Piper and added, "We were just thinking of searching the lakes."

"Not just lakes. Creeks, marshes, swamps," Piper corrected.

Why do you not search the swamp? The boy in the red shirt had said that. Neve sucked in a breath. "Swamps," she repeated.

"Why do we care about swamps?" Sammy said.

Neve and Piper exchanged looks.

"*We* don't," Piper said, and she started to say something else. She was going to tell Sammy to leave them alone, Neve knew.

"There was a fog," Neve interjected. "When Rose disappeared."

"A fog?" As usual, Neve couldn't tell what Sammy's big smile meant. But maybe, Neve thought, it wasn't always possible to tell from people's expressions what they thought of what you were saying. Maybe you just had to try them and see what happened.

She explained. And though Piper had a sour look on her face, Neve told him about Piper's sister too. And the fact that fog had been seen when other girls went missing.

By the time she finished, Sammy was leaning back in a chair, balancing on the back legs. "So this is why you were asking about magic. A swamp, eh? Got it."

Neve and Piper exchanged looks again.

"No," Piper said. "I don't think you've got it."

"What Piper means to say," Neve said, "is that we think this really *is* magic."

"Heard you the first time," Sammy said, flipping a pencil while he balanced there.

The librarian returned, carrying a dish of fragrant lasagna. She eyed Sammy. He set his chair down with a thump.

"Look," Sammy said. "Since you told me that, I'll tell you about a coin."

"We don't have time for a random story," Piper said.

"Come on, Piper. Let's hear it." Neve was getting used to how Sammy sometimes made a point in a roundabout way.

"So, picture this," Sammy said. "My mom has this coin collection she inherited from her dad. All kinds of cool old coins from different countries. When I was little, I wanted to play with them even though I wasn't supposed to. I stole this one coin. It was silver with a gold edge. I used to carry it around. I'd toss it up and catch it when my mom wasn't looking. Once I was doing that while I was waiting on my mom and someone else caught it and wouldn't give it back."

Piper harrumphed. Even Neve was getting impatient. "But does it have something to do with Rose?"

"Hang on. So, I was in the woods just north of where you live when this happened. Mom was scraping some moss off bark or something, and this . . . guy who caught it—well, it wasn't actually a guy—was up in a tree. And he said to me"—and here Sammy adopted a spooky voice—"'I will return your treasure if you enter the place where pine meets thorn and retrieve a treasure for me in turn.'"

"You are totally making this up to mess with us," Piper said. "That is completely rude."

"Yeah, Mom didn't believe me either," Sammy said cheerfully. "She took away my Xbox for losing Papi's coin."

"What do you mean, it wasn't actually a guy?" Neve said.

"He looked like a man but he was all shrunken up, and he crawled . . . well, after he stole my coin, he crawled up the tree *backwards*. I screamed for my mom. I told on myself, I was so scared."

"You're saying a shrunken-up man kidnapped Rose?" Piper said in a way that meant she thought it was a completely ridiculous theory.

"No, what I meant was . . . that's weird, right? Sounds supernatural? And right before he did that, stole my coin, I remember smelling a swamp. It smelled really bad. I could get us to the spot. Or close to it, I think."

Neve's heart gave a lurch. "That boy I told you about. The one who drew the knife. He talked about a swamp last night. He said I needed to go there."

"You didn't tell me that," Piper said, frowning.

"And Mrs. Peterson mentioned a swamp too. She said it was back in the woods near where we live," Neve said.

"Who's Mrs. Peterson?" Piper said, frowning even harder.

"Our bus driver."

"Sounds like a plan," Sammy said. "We look for the swamp."

Neve returned his smile, for once not caring if her braces showed.

Piper studied the two of them. She seemed annoyed. "And *me*. I'm going too."

"You are?" Neve said. She recalled now that the bus driver had *also* said some people had "worried over" a swamp when Piper's sister disappeared. But Piper hadn't mentioned anything about that; maybe Piper hadn't heard that particular rumor. "I thought your parents wouldn't let you out of the house."

"I'll figure that out somehow."

Sammy jumped up. "Mom's got class tonight. I'll work on catching a ride to your house, Neve."

"The ROTC bus was there last night," Neve said, remembering. "I saw high-schoolers searching. Maybe you can ride with them."

"Good thinking." Sammy ran out, passing someone standing in the doorway.

The boy in the red shirt. His grin seemed to say, *Isn't that interesting.* And his teeth . . . Neve gasped . . . his teeth were *definitely* pointed.

Then he stepped back into the hall.

Neve dashed to the door but he was gone. "Did you see that boy? The boy I told you about. He was *right there*."

"Listening to us? That can't be good." Piper was taking something off the printer.

"No, it isn't," Neve said. "What does he want?"

"Here's a map of the area around your house. Did you tell the police about him?"

"I told my mom he'd been on the bus." Neve unzipped her backpack to put in the map, and there was the fairy-tale book. "Ugh, why did my mom put this creepy book in my backpack?"

"Can I see it?" Piper said.

Neve handed it over. "We found it in the house we're renting."

The bell rang; lunch period was over.

"It's not from the library, that's for sure," Piper said. "Okay if I borrow it?"

Neve nodded. She should have told Mom about the boy in the woods, she thought. And the things he'd said.

"Time to head to class," the librarian called from her desk.

"Yes, ma'am," Piper said, gathering her books and papers.

"Can I use your phone?" Neve said. "I want to tell my mom about the swamp. Maybe the police know where it is."

Mom answered right away.

By the time Neve finished telling her everything, she and Piper had moved out into the hallway and the warning bell was ringing. Neve could barely hear Mom over the bell and the kids.

"It's a lot to take in, honey," Mom said. "I mean . . . shrunken men in trees?"

"You don't believe me," Neve said.

"I'm trying to. I know you wouldn't make things up. I'm wondering if you and your friends might be confused on a few of the details—"

"There's another thing. I felt something, Mom. A pain in my mouth. It was like that time Rose broke her arm. You need to tell the police to search for the swamp."

A pause. "Where's this swamp supposed to be again?"

"Sammy thought it was in the woods just north of us. That's kind of what the bus driver said too."

"That's funny. I don't remember the real estate agent mentioning a swamp. Tell you what—Dad's just getting back with the dogs and their handlers. They think maybe they'll find something, thanks to the shoe. While the dogs are resting, Dad and I will just take a little peek in the woods. No stone unturned, right?"

"No, Mom, it's dangerous. Didn't you hear what I said? You need to bring the detective."

"He's busy right now, but don't worry. If we see anything suspicious, we'll tell him."

"Don't go in there, not without the police," Neve said. The hall was clearing out.

"I know it's hard for you not to worry," Mom said. "But you need to try. It'll take only a minute, and I'll call the school the second we know anything. Go to class now, sweetie."

"*Mom*—oh no. She hung up."

"Call back," Piper said.

Neve tried calling back. It went straight to voice mail.

They stared at each other. The last of the kids scurried into classrooms. Neve and Piper were the only ones left in the hall. The final bell rang.

"We don't have hall passes." Neve felt light-headed, like she had left her body and was looking down at herself from somewhere in the vicinity of the smoke detector.

"What are you going to do?" Piper said.

How to trust her own gut? Neve tried to listen, and oddly, her gut seemed to be telling her something about the math teacher. "Mr. Adams," she said aloud.

"Um, I don't think he'd be much help," Piper said. "He's too indecisive. I've been behind him in the lunch line. If the cafeteria has both hamburgers and nachos, it's excruciating."

"I don't exactly need him, but . . . Mr. Adams rides his bike to school, right?"

"I think so," Piper said. "Why?"

"I'm going."

The light reflected off Piper's glasses. "Just, like, leaving? You don't need anyone else. You work alone, then?"

"No, it's not that. I need your help. But I have a bad feeling about this. I can't wait until after school to check on Mom."

"Okay, then," Piper said. "I'll cover you."

"Cover me?"

"The front doors are the only ones that aren't alarmed. They just beep. Follow me."

"But what about Miss Terry?" Neve said.

"Let me take care of it." Piper marched to the front desk and announced, "Miss Terry, I drank milk and might be having a *severe* allergic reaction. I'm going to need to start screaming."

"Screaming? Why would you—Piper! Come back here! We'll get the nurse." Miss Terry zoomed her wheelchair toward the nurse's office.

Piper's screaming started then, and the *beep* of Neve exiting the front doors was drowned out.

Mr. Adams's bike was exactly where it was every morning, in the rack out front. The lock was propped up, since it didn't actually work. Neve had noticed it was never quite closed.

"Sorry, Mr. Adams," she said as she wheeled the bike to the curb. "But this is an emergency."

Pushing hard on the pedals, she left the parking lot quickly and passed through the small downtown, where there was hardly any traffic, to the roads beyond. She hadn't been biking all that long when she smelled the scent carried by a strange wind coming from the direction of the woods, the direction of her house: musty attics, secret cupboards, hidden doors that were creaking open.

It smelled of magic.

Chapter Eighteen

A MIST IN THE DISTANCE.

Neve turned onto the state road and saw it, hovering over the trees, right above where her house should be. She stood on the pedals, pushing the bike to go faster. All the cycling and the press of her backpack made sweat trickle between her shoulder blades.

Was it the fog? Her heart pounded in her ears.

Closer now, she could see it wasn't like before. It wasn't a thick, rolling fog. This mist was light and thin, much more spread out. It covered her house and everything around it: The line of buses, the police vehicles, the people walking around. A truck with a motorboat hitched to it. A jeep with a trailer that smelled like dogs and declared itself to be CAROLINA SEARCH, TRACK, AND RESCUE. The mist covered it all. Neve cycled right into it. It was cold against her cheeks.

Neve leaned the bike against the house. Two pairs of muddy boots were by the back door. "Mom, are you here?"

Mom was there. She was in the kitchen, at the sink.

"I know I shouldn't have left school by myself," Neve said, "but I wanted to be sure . . ."

Mom turned around. "Why, hello there, daughter. Would you like some refreshment?"

Neve forgot what she was going to say.

Mom's hair was poufy, like she'd curled it with hot rollers. She also had on makeup, though she hadn't done a good job with it. Smudged black spots were around her eyes; she looked like she'd been using mascara but had missed her eyelashes. By a lot.

"Why do you look like that?" Neve said. "Did something happen?"

"You've had a long day," Mom said. "I shall fix you a steaming roast with beans."

"I haven't had a long day. I'm home early, remember? I came home by myself. Why aren't you mad about that?" The kitchen was just coming into focus. Flour was strewn around. The drawer with the dish towels had been emptied onto the floor. Mom's extensive cookbook collection was in odd little stacks, arranged by color. If this was a new sort of cleaning project, it made no sense to Neve.

"Mothers are nurturing. Mothers do not get angry," Mom said.

"Yes, you do. You're supposed to. If I do something wrong." Neve took a step backwards. "Did you go to the swamp? Did something happen?"

"Oho! Full-grown persons cannot go to the swamp. That is not allowed. If you try to send another, she says, the consequences will be severe." Mom's expression was oddly blank.

"What? Who is *she*? Who said that?" Neve said.

Mom blinked. "Who said what? What about biscuits and gravy? That would be scrumptious, don't you think? I'm sure you're starving." Mom smiled then, a strange little smile that didn't travel to her eyes.

Mom never made biscuits and gravy. She didn't think it was healthy. Plus, when Mom made biscuits with almond flour, the way Neve needed them because of her allergy, she described them as "biscuits that are a little nutty" (and always laughed).

"Sure," Neve said, edging toward the door. "I'm so hungry I could eat a horse *and* its saddle."

"Is that humor?" Mom said.

Neve turned and ran outside. Felt the mist against her skin. "Dad! Dad!"

Dad stood at the corner of the house facing the brick. He wore no shoes.

"Dad?" Neve said.

He turned around. The lenses of his glasses were cracked, and the mist had fogged them. "Hello there, second daughter. First daughter is gone, you know. She won't be coming back."

Dad would *never* have said those words like that.

Neve backed away, jumped onto the bike, and started pedaling. Not that she knew where she was going.

The detective was getting into a sedan. He looked leaner than ever, hollows in his cheeks.

"Detective Rogers!" she said.

He paused with the driver's-side door open.

"Something's wrong with Mom and Dad," Neve said. "The swamp did something to them, I think. Mom said that *she* said the consequences would be severe. Mom was talking about someone. I don't know who."

"Sometimes things just happen." The detective's hair was sticking to that hollow face; it was like the mist had settled in it.

"What?"

"We can't always fix everything. As much as we'd like to. Try not to be too sad." He got into the sedan. Started the car. Drove away.

Everyone was driving away: The police vehicles. The truck and trailers. The buses. People were lining up to board the last few. All of them inside the fine mist.

Neve pedaled to the street. An older man stood in line for the Ebenezer Baptist bus. "Why are you leaving?" Neve said.

"Sometimes things just happen. And there's nothing we can do about it." The man climbed onto the bus, and it departed with the others.

Neve's stomach was tying itself up in knots and double knots. The hound nudged her leg.

"Where have you been?" she said. "We've got a disaster on our hands."

The hound had no comment. But he waited while she took Piper's map out of her backpack.

"I'm going to find the swamp. I'm going to find Rose." Neve

turned the map upside down, then sideways. It was a topographical map and hard to read, but she didn't see a swamp anywhere nearby. "Oh, let's just get started and we'll see."

When Neve began pedaling again, he followed, loping easily beside the bike. "This is horrible. This is horrible," she kept repeating. "And don't you think I should know your name at a time like this?"

The hound didn't answer. Someone else did.

"Bear. Fancy seeing you here."

A woman was right in front of Neve.

Neve swerved, skidded on the bike, and crashed into the weeds at the side of the road.

The woman hadn't been there a second earlier, Neve could have sworn it. She scrambled to her feet.

The woman was old. Or maybe not. She was a little too perfect-looking, with no wrinkles, blue eyes pale as winter. She wore an old-fashioned black dress with a white collar. She looked like a portrait of herself. And even more disturbing, she stood inside a mass of fog that covered most of her legs.

"Ready to come back and hunt game for me again, Bear?" The woman was talking to the hound.

The hound, though, was looking at Neve.

"Who are you?" Neve said.

"I think you know." The woman's teeth were very white.

"What do you mean?" Neve said.

"What do *you* mean?"

Neve didn't know exactly what was going on, but she knew what she meant to do. "I mean . . . to find my sister."

"She's already in a pine box, my pet. I'm sorry to be the one to tell you." The woman did not look sorry. If anything, her smile grew wider. She made a circle with her hand, and the fog seemed to respond to the movement, swirling and spinning. On the white-gray surface, right in front of Neve, an image of Rose appeared, hunched up and crammed inside what appeared to be a square wooden box. Rose wasn't moving.

Neve's heart was in her throat. "She's dead?"

"She's gone. And if you try to find her, I'll make a box for you too," the woman said. "And for anyone *else* you send along."

No, no, no. This couldn't be right. It couldn't be. And Neve couldn't let this woman get to her. "So you're saying it was you," Neve said. "It was you who took Rose. It was you who did something to Mom and Dad."

"Is that really what you want to know? Or do you want to know why I took your sister instead of *you?*"

Neve froze. She couldn't think of a single reply.

The woman gave an exaggerated shrug. "Sometimes things just happen." And she spread her arms wide, and the fog expanded upward to engulf her and that knowing smile. Then there was a sound like the cracking of a whip, and a ribbon of fog wrapped around the dog. He disappeared with a small *yip!*

The fog began to take in the mist covering Neve's house. Like an oversize sponge, the fog absorbed the mist, bit by hazy bit, growing larger and larger, fatter and fatter, until the entirety of the mist was inside it, and the bloated mass of white fog was as big as a house, as big as a giant.

"Why have you done this?" Neve shouted up at it.

The mass of fog hung there for a moment, looming over her, whispering, like it was considering her.

Then it collapsed like a great ocean wave, flattened, and flowed into the trees. To the right, to the left. Neve couldn't tell the direction it headed.

"Get back here!" Neve said. She didn't know if she was speaking to the fog or the woman.

Neither of them came back.

And they'd taken the hound too.

Chapter Nineteen

NEVE'S BOX DIDN'T feel cozy and safe the way it usually did.

It felt small and tight and suffocating.

She was sitting in the box in her bedroom with the door closed. *I can't do this by myself, I can't,* she thought. *I can't do it.*

Neve was *not quite enough* by herself. She needed Rose. She couldn't *be* without Rose. Rose propped her up, made her what she was. This could not have happened, it could not have—

Mom's cell phone rang for the third time.

The first two times, Neve had ignored it. But this time, she crawled out of the darkness of her box, went out into the hall, and located the cell phone on the hall table.

Mom was not around to answer it. That was because she and Dad were crouched in the planting bed outside next to the rose-bushes. They cried over the drooping bushes as if they were the saddest things they'd ever seen, even when Neve stood right in front of them and shouted at them to talk to her. They just kept saying, "Our babies," and their hands bled because they kept touching the thorns.

Neve didn't recognize the number on the phone. "Hello?"

"Finally!" someone said.

"Is this Piper?" Neve said.

"Of course it's Piper. What took you so long?"

Neve shrugged, not that Piper could see that. "How'd you get this number?"

"You used my phone to call your mom earlier, silly," Piper said. "Anyway, I've been looking at this book and I think someone gave it to you for a reason."

"What book?"

"The fairy-tale book. The old one. What is the matter with you?"

"Something is wrong with Mom and Dad. And there was this mist that covered everything. Everyone left. No one is looking for Rose anymore."

"Oh no," Piper said. "What's wrong with your parents?"

"I don't know," Neve said. "They're just acting really weird. But it's because of the woman. She said that Rose was . . . that Rose was . . ." She couldn't finish.

"What woman?"

Neve described her. "I've never seen her before. But she was with the fog. I believe what she said. She told me not to try and find Rose. That Rose was already in a . . . pine box. Then the woman disappeared into the fog, just like Rose did."

A long pause. Neve could hear Piper breathing.

"Here's a fact," Piper said finally. "You don't spray tomato vines for fruitworms if you've already harvested the tomatoes."

"Um, okay," Neve said. "What?"

"What I mean is, why would she bother warning you off if it was already too late?"

Neve thought about that. "That's true. Maybe she was lying to get me to stop looking. And it worked!"

"Almost worked," Piper said. "The situation isn't hopeless yet. Which brings me back around to this book."

"Yes?" Neve said, standing taller and bouncing on her toes.

"Do you remember the page where the girls are wondering if their mother will sacrifice another daughter? It's page twenty-three, with the picture of the trees."

"No, not really," Neve said. She'd tried to forget about the book, actually.

"I've been looking at it since Bubba picked me up. It's been bothering me all afternoon. It's got these three cypress trees and this statue of a girl?"

"Okay," Neve said. The picture sounded familiar.

"I recognize those trees and that statue. It took me a while to place it. But I've seen trees like this and a girl statue over near where I used to live, where *you* live. The trees are in a graveyard next to a white church with a picket fence around it. The building is boarded up. There's a little gravel road that goes into the graveyard. Do you remember?"

Neve did remember. At least, she remembered the church and the graveyard, if not the statue. "Maybe the book was a clue! Maybe that's where Rose is."

"I'm on my way," Piper said.

"Meet me at the church," Neve said. "And text Sammy too."

156

She shoved a water bottle and box of granola bars into her backpack. Then she grabbed a jacket that hung by the back door. It was white denim and she didn't much like it, but she was in a hurry.

"Bye, Mom," she said. "Bye, Dad."

"Our babies," Mom and Dad cried. But they weren't really talking to her, Neve knew.

A pang in her heart. After she found Rose, Neve would have to fix Mom and Dad. "Don't worry. I'm going to do it. I'm going to figure it out," she said, pedaling hard up the drive. It was early evening, maybe six. The wind rustled the leaves in the trees.

"She's alive, isn't she?" Neve asked the trees. "She must be. I would know it otherwise."

The wind tugged at her backpack. It blew toward the church.

Neve took that as a yes. "Thank you," she said and pedaled furiously in that direction.

* * *

Not too many minutes later, Neve arrived. The wooden sign in front, which had fallen and was covered in dirt, read REDHILL CHURCH. Though there wasn't a hill, red or otherwise. Everything was flat. She pedaled onto the gravel drive that led to the gravestones and soon recognized the three large cypress trees from the picture in the book.

The trees had been planted in a triangle, and in the center of the triangle was the statue, just like Piper had said. A small tree with yellow leaves hung over the statue protectively, like a little yellow umbrella.

Neve leaned the bike against a tree and went to take a look.

Dark with age, the statue was of a long-haired girl, maybe a teenager, in a flowing dress. She was on her knees, gazing into the distance, hands tied behind her back. The statue was altogether more disturbing than Neve remembered from the illustration in the book, where the tied hands had not been shown.

She pulled the weeds away from the base. An inscription: REMEMBER. It told her nothing other than that someone had been sorry the girl died.

Neve sat back on her heels.

She was in a graveyard. Where people were buried. The woman had talked about Rose being in a pine box, which Neve had taken to mean a coffin. Could Rose be buried here? Was that what the clue meant?

The thought made the air catch in Neve's lungs. What if Rose was buried alive? Neve jumped up and began to sprint around the graveyard, calling out for Rose, tripping on the markers. But after a few minutes of panicked running, she slowed.

Fresh dirt, she thought.

She'd not seen any of that. Surely fresh dirt would be around a newly dug grave. She took a breath and inspected the graveyard more carefully. It wasn't very large.

No, not even an overturned clod. There weren't any flowers, fresh or otherwise, no signs that the graves had been visited recently.

Maybe the picture in the book hadn't meant anything at all.

She knelt in front of the statue. If she remembered right, the illustration had shown only the three trees and the statue. Not the tree with the yellow leaves, not the rest of the graveyard, and not the church. So maybe that meant it was the trees or the statue that was important.

The statue girl looked like someone who'd been captured. Neve stood, walked to the rear of the statue, and looked at the hands again. Yes, that was definitely supposed to be rope.

"Neve!" Sammy rolled up on a rickety skateboard with a green pack on his back. "Sorry it took me so long. I haven't skated in forever and these wheels are pretty rusty. The ROTC bus wasn't coming. They were going to pizza night instead. I don't get it."

"I think it was the mist," Neve said.

"Mist?"

"Long story."

A black Subaru drove up and idled on the gravel road. The back door opened and Piper stepped out, also wearing a backpack.

"A rideshare," Piper explained as the car drove away. "I used Bubba's credit card. I know I'm going to pay for that. And I don't mean with my allowance. I mean with blood. I told him I was going back to my room to work on the computer and then I turned location services off on my phone and climbed out the window. He's going to realize soon I'm not home. And if I don't get killed out here, Bubba and Pops are going to do it."

"Are you sure you should have come?" Neve said.

"There are ten thousand varieties of tomato around the world. Tomato seedlings are even grown in space. Think about that."

"Um . . ." Neve said.

"For sure I should have come," Piper said. "This is big. This is everything."

She meant her own sister, Neve realized. Piper thought she might find her sister too. "I'm glad you did," Neve said.

"Thanks." And then, turning to Sammy, Piper said, "And don't think I don't know why you're here. Don't think I don't know why you're helping."

It was a surprisingly mean thing to say. Piper hadn't even said hello to him.

"Aww, I just want to help." Sammy kicked a loose piece of gravel. And then, as if he wanted to distract Piper, he said, "There's a weeping redbud." The small tree with the yellow leaves. "Somebody planted that there on purpose. You don't see them everywhere."

Neve was happy to change the subject. She didn't know what was going on with Piper. "Really? Maybe someone was trying to hide the statue."

"Or make sure people noticed it," Sammy said. "Those leaves are really bright. And the flowers in the spring are even more noticeable, a lavender color."

"It's the sister who was traded for the cup," Piper said.

"What?" Neve said.

"If we assume for a minute that the story is true," Piper said.

"What story?" Sammy said.

A true fairy tale? Neve hadn't considered that. But the boy in the red shirt and the woman with the fog . . . "Did you bring it?"

Piper took the book from her backpack. Neve turned to the page with the statue, and Sammy looked over her shoulder.

Would she sacrifice another daughter for more magic to extend her beauty and her life? read the text below the illustration of the three trees and the statue.

"Pretty evil to sacrifice your kid," Sammy said. "Fits the profile of a kidnapper."

"If we assume it's true, this would be the daughter that was traded away," Piper said, touching the statue.

Neve flipped to the beginning of the book.

She took a great ship to a desolate land and went to live alone in a boggy wood.

"A swamp."

"We're on the right track," Sammy said.

Piper paid no attention to them; she'd obviously already made those connections. "But she's tied up. That doesn't make sense. Most people want to remember the best moments about their loved ones, when they were the most brave or beautiful or whatever. They don't make statues of them with bullet wounds or with their heads chopped off. To make a statue of her tied up meant that someone didn't want anyone to forget what happened to her. Or maybe that *does* make sense. It's good not to forget." She glared at Sammy but he didn't look at her. Instead, he scratched his forearm.

"That's a good point," Neve said, glancing between the two

of them. "Just so you know, I did look for clues around this area. But no one has been here in a long time."

"You mean this was a wasted trip?" Piper said.

"We can still go look for the swamp," Sammy said. "Like we planned."

"We need something else to go on. What if we can't find the right swamp? There are swamps everywhere. And it's so late. It's going to be dark soon." Piper sighed heavily.

Neve wasn't ready to give up. "The inscription is one word: *Remember*," she said. "So it's true that whoever put it here didn't want people to forget her."

Piper frowned. "That's it? Not her name? Seems like they'd put her name. How could anyone remember her without a name?"

Neve knelt next to the statue. It was life-size. If the figure hadn't been up on the pedestal, Neve and the girl would have been the same height. Neve put her hands behind her back and tried to imagine how the girl must have felt. She must've been sad, being separated from her family. She also might've been cold; she wore only a thin dress. The girl gazed into the distance. What was she looking at?

Neve followed the statue's line of sight. A brief spark of light, and the sunset burned yellow on two objects back along the road. Objects that had *not* been there only a moment before. She sucked in a breath. "Look," she said.

"More of the weeping redbuds," Sammy said. "That's no accident."

The small yellow trees were back along the road Neve had cycled. She must've gone right past them and hadn't noticed. "Let's go see. Maybe there are more statues," Neve said.

That seemed to cheer Piper up. "A lead!"

Neve ran to the bike. *This could be it!*

But she couldn't leap onto the bike and take off, since Piper wanted to come but didn't want to ride on the handlebars. She'd never done that before, she said. It might be risky. So Neve walked the bike toward the trees.

"Where was the mist?" Piper said. "What was it like?"

"It was all around my house," Neve said. "It covered everything. It seemed like regular mist but it was the fog. Everyone kept saying *These things happen* and then they just left. They stopped searching."

"I knew it," Piper said. "Magic was making them forget. I don't remember the mist after Jannie left, but it had to be there. I bet it covered the town too. But it doesn't work on us. Hmm."

"Um, mist?" Sammy said.

Neve filled Sammy in on everything as they walked.

* * *

No statues were beneath the yellow-leaved trees, although they flanked the entrance to an old country road. A road of dirt and stone that was narrow and twisting and surrounded by tall pines that blocked what remained of the light. There were no signs of any sort, nothing like BEWARE or DANGER.

Not that there was any need for signs. Everything about the area screamed *Beware*.

"Check that road out!" Sammy said. "I almost didn't see it there."

"I go this way every day on the bus," Neve said, "and I've never noticed it."

Piper shrugged. "Magic. I told you. This road wasn't on any map I looked at. I would have remembered. Therefore, it's got to be where we need to go."

The road is in plain sight, but only a child can see it. The boy in the red shirt had said that. But how did he know? "I think you're right," Neve said.

"Let's hope the magic road doesn't disappear while we're walking on it," Sammy said cheerily.

The road was really dark. Neve remembered one of the stories the kids told: that if you walked into the woods, you'd be swallowed up. And the woman with the fog had told her as much: *If you try to find her, I'll make a box for you too.* The box part was actually kind of ironic, Neve realized.

"She threatened me," Neve said. "Told me not to come after Rose, not to send anyone else. You two should go back." Though she didn't want them to. She didn't want to go in alone.

"Aww, I'm not afraid of any foggy lady," Sammy said. "Besides, my mom's class goes late. We've got plenty of time to find Rose and get back before she comes home. I won't get grounded."

"I'm not talking about getting *grounded*," Neve said. "I'm talking about getting *dead*."

"I don't care about the danger. I'm going," Piper said and marched onto the road.

"Wait for us!" Sammy said.

Chapter Twenty

TWILIGHT WAS TURNING to dusk as Neve, Sammy, and Piper walked the road beneath the towering pines. Sammy lit the way. He was the only one who'd thought to bring a flashlight. They left the bike and skateboard behind, since even if they'd had more light, the road was too rocky and uneven for riding.

"The trees don't like it here," Neve said, then wished she hadn't. It was an odd thing to say.

But Sammy seemed to consider it. "Maybe they don't." As they walked, he explained that his mom was doing her PhD dissertation on trees and how they shift their ranges over time to places where they can grow well. "Except when they can't migrate. Like when their seeds are blocked by acres of concrete or lakes or farmland or something."

"But there's nothing blocking them here," Neve said.

"That we can see," Piper said ominously.

Sammy had been scanning the trees as he spoke. He pointed the flashlight upward. "Did you notice how tall these pines are? I've never seen pines this tall."

They *were* tall. The first limbs were at least twenty feet up.

"I'm going to try and take a picture for my mom," he said and took out his cell phone. "Scratch that. It's too dark. Hey, I don't have a signal here."

"We lost cell service when we stepped onto this road," Piper said. "I would have mentioned it except I didn't want to interrupt your important discussion about seeds."

Sammy ignored the second part of her comment. "Why would there be a dead spot here?"

"Not gonna say it again," Piper said.

"Okay, no big deal. I'm going to mark this, though." Sammy knelt and made a little pile of rocks. "This is called a cairn. Or a duck. It's how park rangers mark trails for hikers."

"We're on a road," Piper said. "We don't need a stack of stones to mark the path."

"Piper, let's hear what he's thinking," Neve said. "Sammy, why *would* you need to mark it?"

"Since this is a magic road, I'm going to treat this like a dangerous place. We might need some help getting out. I've also brought the backpack I took out with Mom all those times. I've got everything in here. So we're good."

"Everything?" Neve said as they started walking again.

"Like a survival kit and stuff. The medicine's probably expired, though."

"Why do you sound so cheerful about it?" Piper said.

"No use in being a grump."

Piper harrumphed. Grumpily.

Neve strained her eyes in the direction of her house, or where she thought her house should be. She'd left a ton of lights on and she ought to be able to see it. But she could not. She looked back for the pile of rocks but couldn't see that either. It was hard to see much of anything outside of where Sammy pointed the flashlight. It suddenly seemed like a very good idea to have the little rock pile. "Where are the rocks again?"

"Right there . . ." Sammy swung the beam around. "Hey, where'd they go? We've only walked, like, ten feet." He searched with the flashlight for some time.

The pile of rocks was gone.

"Guess we walked farther than I realized." He took a bright orange ribbon from his pack and tied it around a tree trunk. "I hate to use these because they're plastic, but we'll be able to see them better." He scratched his arm.

"That's good," Neve said, glancing into the dark of the woods. When she and Rose camped out in a tent in the backyard of the old house, Neve took the sleeping bag near the flap door, pretending the dark didn't bother her. But here . . . the silent trees seemed to press ever nearer, as if they were looking over her shoulder. The dark was different here.

"We're wasting time," Piper said. "Let's keep going."

Neve forced her eyes to the road in front of her. And they stayed close together as the road curved through the forest.

After a while, Sammy said, "Check it out," and flashed the light onto a greenish growth on a fallen tree.

"We care about lichen why?" Piper said.

"Fungi and algae. A type of mutualism where one can't get

along without the other." He sounded extra-cheerful, as if he was trying hard to lighten the mood.

"Oh, yeah," Neve said, playing along. "As opposed to those that can exist independently."

"Basic stuff," Piper said. "Everybody knows that." She brushed past them.

Piper felt left out, Neve thought. The way Neve had felt at the lunch table when Bets sat in her spot. And what if Neve had *never* had a spot to sit in? Was that what it was like for Piper? Neve pictured herself wandering around the cafeteria with no one to call out to her, no one to ask her to sit next to them. It wasn't a good feeling.

She followed behind Piper without commenting.

When they walked around the next bend, Sammy's flashlight caught a house. Or what used to be a house. Moss covered the windows, and the brick chimney looked like it'd been smashed with a giant fist. The house was slumped over as if it were sinking, the ground devouring it.

"I guess no one lives *there*," Neve said.

A baby doll, grimy and ancient-looking, lay on the drive. Blue eyes stared at them.

"Spooky," Sammy said. "I'm sure not touching that."

"It's just an old doll," Piper said. "And no one asked you to touch it."

"Come on, you've got to admit that's spooky," Sammy said.

Neve said, "It *is* spooky."

"There are spookier things ahead, I bet," Piper said.

They quickly passed the doll. Then Sammy flashed the light behind them. "Maybe not."

The doll seemed to be watching them.

"Did that doll . . . turn?" Neve said.

"It was facing the other way before. It was!" Sammy said.

They watched it for a full minute while Neve's heart thumped in her chest.

It didn't move.

Of course it didn't move.

"You're just trying to scare us," Piper said.

"Me?" Sammy said. "I've been walking with you the whole time. You would have seen me if I'd moved that doll."

"You like upsetting people. You do. Everybody knows it was you who made Morgan Nichols cry," Piper said.

"No, I don't like upsetting people. And I didn't mean to do that," Sammy said.

"Morgan Nichols?" Neve said.

"One of the girls I told you about," Piper said. "One of the girls who disappeared and people forgot. Sammy made fun of the birthmark on her face and she cried hysterically in the bathroom. She disappeared a week later."

"I didn't forget her. And I didn't mean to make fun of her either," Sammy said. "My mouth used to get ahead of my brain. I'm not like that anymore. I went to a counselor." He scratched his arm.

"You're just here because you feel guilty," Piper said.

"That's not why. I want to find Rose, same as you," Sammy said.

"Didn't you say it was a long time ago that that girl disappeared?" Neve said.

"Three years," Piper said. "Three long years."

Even if Sammy had been mean to that girl, he was younger then, Neve thought. People change.

"And you said that I was getting into too many cookies," Piper said to Sammy. "And that I looked like a leprechaun."

Sammy scratched some more. "I don't remember that. I'm sorry. I didn't mean it." He sounded like he might cry.

"When was that?" Neve said.

"It was first grade," Piper said. "It was terrible."

If Rose were here, she would stop this in a second. She'd say something outrageous or funny or demanding and have them laughing. But Rose was not there. And there was no one else to do it.

"You realize Sammy was, like, *six* in first grade," Neve said. "You're actually still mad about stuff he did when he was *six*? And Sammy, what's wrong with your arm?"

"Eczema. It's no big deal. Though I'm not supposed to scratch."

"Let's just focus on what we're doing," Neve said. "Maybe we should put up another one of those markers, what do you think?"

"Sure thing!" Sammy got another ribbon out of his backpack.

Neve could feel Piper's eyes on her in the dark, but Piper didn't say anything.

Taking charge wasn't so bad, actually. Neve had done more talking and deciding in the past two days than she'd ever done in her life. Maybe being assertive and making decisions were skills that you got better at the more you practiced them, like her forehand swing in tennis. It was something to think about.

They continued on, walking single file as the road narrowed even further, Sammy first, with the light, then Neve, then Piper. The trees were noiseless and still, the feel of them stifling. Sammy kept flashing the light into them. Looking for that shrunken-up man, Neve thought. Though he didn't mention it.

"Jannie was the smart one," Piper said suddenly.

Neve started. "The smart one of who?"

"The smart one of the two of us. She would've figured this all out right away."

Neve sincerely doubted that. She'd never met anyone as smart as Piper. "You think?"

"I was the stubborn one. Though Bubba says I'm *persistent*. Also, the messy one."

"Rose is the leader. I'm the follower," Neve said. She'd overheard Coach Ellen saying that. "Also, I'm the quiet one and Rose is the loud one." That *everyone* said.

"Huh," Piper said. "The quiet one, I get. Not so sure about the follower one."

"I'm the quiet one *and* the loud one," Sammy announced. "The leader *and* the follower. Benefits of being an only child. I can be everything!"

A lot of things to try to be all by yourself, Neve thought.

Mom was always telling Neve she could be anything she wanted. But how was that even possible? Was she supposed to just wake up one morning and make a list?

"No, you're definitely the loud one. Shouldn't we keep it down?" Piper said to Sammy. "And that pothole looks like the same one we passed ten minutes ago."

"It can't be," Neve said as Sammy put the light on it. "We would have known if we were walking in circles."

"Wonder how long we've been . . . that's weird, the clock on my phone isn't working either," Sammy said.

Scratch-scratch.

The sound came from behind them.

Neve froze. "Are you doing that?"

"Not me," Sammy said, swinging the flashlight around.

Bare, empty road, covered in shadows.

"Should we go back?" Piper said.

"Back *toward* the sound?" Neve said.

"Go on the offense," Piper said. "Surprise it."

"*It?*" Neve stared at the road behind. She suspected they were all imagining the doll following them, creeping along the ground with those little arms, though she didn't want to say it out loud.

"Yeah, I say go forward," Sammy said. "Let *it* alone."

"Okay, but what about we put up another marker?" Piper said.

"Great idea!" Sammy put another orange ribbon on a tree while Piper swept the light around, checking for the source of the sound.

Nothing revealed itself. And the sound didn't come again.

When they calmed down and were ready to continue, Sammy said to Neve, "You glow in the dark, did you know? Kinda like a ghost."

"Yeah, I've been told that." It was her hair. In the dark, it seemed to reflect any light. Even starlight. Maybe her skin too. Everyone at camp last summer seemed to think it was hilarious. Everyone except Rose.

"I thought you said you didn't do that anymore, Sammy," Piper said.

"What?" Sammy said. "That wasn't an insult."

"It's not, it's fine," Neve said. "Though I wish I'd worn a hoodie. And not this white jacket. I'm like a walking light bulb."

"Ha," Sammy said. "A talented artist and funny too."

Sammy was being extra-nice in case he'd hurt her feelings, Neve knew. But Mom *had* always said she was funny. Mom, who had bought this jacket for her and a similar one in blue for Rose. Mom had seen them and thought of her daughters at once, she said. That was because red and white roses were embroidered on the backs. Rose had hated hers on sight. They weren't very cute jackets; even Neve could see that. But she wore hers sometimes so as not to hurt Mom's feelings.

Neve suddenly imagined Mom finding her and Rose in pine boxes, Neve wearing the jacket over her dead and decomposing body. Mom would be so sad. Or maybe it'd be worse if she was *never* able to find them. Mom might end up dusting and vacuuming night after night, unable to stop because she'd never found out what had happened to her daughters.

Neve wished she'd thought to leave a note.

"I just realized something," Piper said. "If that statue was really the sister from the book, the one who was traded to the dwarves, that means the other two sisters are probably the ones who have Rose."

"I only saw one woman," Neve said.

"You probably didn't notice the other one because you were so scared."

"I wasn't so scared that my eyes didn't work. There was only one woman on the road."

"Well, okay. In any case, they're murderers, the both of them," Piper said.

The thought of the woman on the road made Neve's stomach hurt. "Is that flashlight getting dimmer?" she said to Sammy.

"It can't be. I just put new batteries in it," Sammy said.

But the light *was* getting dimmer.

"We'll have to go back," Sammy said finally. "We won't be able to keep going without light."

"We can use the flashlight on your phone," Neve said.

"Yes, we can!" Sammy said.

"NASA left twelve and a half million tomato seeds in space for six years," Piper said. "Out there, in all that dark. When NASA took them back, they were still good. They still grew tomato vines."

"What's that got to do with anything?" Sammy said. "Why are you always talking about tomatoes?"

"Tomatoes are the world's most popular fruit. More popular than bananas!" Piper said.

Piper's obsession with tomatoes, Neve thought, had something to do with her sister. "Tomatoes are pretty cool," Neve said and hoped that Sammy would let it go.

A pause. "Okay, yeah," Sammy said. "I like a good tomato. Like, you can't beat a Margherita pizza."

"We have to be brave like tomato seeds," Piper said. "If we go back, I won't be able to search anymore. Pops must have flipped out by now. Bubba will try to comfort him but it won't work."

"At least they care what you're doing," Sammy said.

"What? Your mom doesn't care what you're doing?" Piper said.

"Sure she does," Sammy said. "She's just really busy. It's hard to run a business and finish a PhD at the same time."

"I would love for my dads to try and get PhDs," Piper said. "Then they wouldn't be into *my* business all the time."

Sammy said nothing. He might, Neve thought, want his mom to get a little more into his business.

They kept walking.

Scratch-scratch.

The sound again. Neve's heart nearly stopped.

"Was that closer?" Piper said.

"Yes, it was," Neve said. "Higher too."

Sammy ran his cell phone light over the trees while they all held their breath. They saw nothing.

"Let's pick up the pace," Sammy said, and he scratched his arm again. "Get away from it." He trained the light on the road ahead, and the three of them bunched so close together, they were treading on each other's shoes and tripping each other up as they rushed around the next few curves.

Sammy stopped abruptly. Neve and Piper ran into him.

"Do you see it?" Sammy said.

A pine tree with orange ribbons around it. Three of them.

"They might not be yours," Piper said.

"One of them was shorter because I tore it too soon, and, see, that bottom one is short," Sammy said. "Those are my ribbons."

They continued to stare.

"She doesn't want us to get out of here," Sammy said. "She doesn't want us to ever leave."

His cell phone rang and they all jumped.

"What?" Sammy said. "I don't have any bars . . ." He listened. "It's for you." He handed the phone to Neve.

"This exercise is pointless," a woman said. Neve knew the voice. It was the woman she had seen on the road. The one with the fog. The one who'd said Rose was in a box.

"Why?" Neve said.

"I have told you."

Neve found Piper's gaze in the night. Why would the woman have called if it was actually pointless? "I don't believe you," Neve said. "I don't believe you've harvested your tomatoes."

"Speaking nonsense will not help your cause," the woman said.

"What difference does it make if I speak nonsense or not?" Neve said.

"You will not get in. There is no way in."

"We'll see," Neve said. The call ended and she returned the phone to Sammy. "It was her."

"We heard," Piper said. "Was it the same one you saw on the road?" When Neve said it was, Piper said, "How can you be sure?"

"Piper, I'm sure," Neve said. "She might have a sister, but the woman on the phone was the one I saw. I recognized her voice."

"Sorry. I'm not very good at letting things go sometimes."

"Is that right?" Sammy said. He was inspecting the trees again with the cell phone light.

"It's okay," Neve said to Piper.

"This means we've gone the right way, you know," Piper said. "She wouldn't have called otherwise."

"But I still don't have any bars," Sammy said. "How'd she call?"

"Told you before," Piper said.

"But technology, though. That's messed up," Sammy said.

They started walking again.

A long time passed without scary noises or mysterious phone calls. Neve began to relax. The three of them shared food and water from their packs. They ate all the granola bars Neve had brought.

Piper said, "Neve, before you moved out here, did you get an ad about the rental in the mail? A flyer that looked old-timey?"

"Yeah, we did. It had big, old-fashioned words on it, I remember, like *endeavors* and *youngsters*."

"We did too. And Pops was so excited about the price. It was her, I know it. She targeted us. We were here because she chose us. But why us?"

Neve thought about that. "I don't know."

They rounded a curve. The moon had risen above the trees.

"Oh! The moon is red," Neve said.

"The blood moon," Piper said. "A total eclipse where the moon is reddish because the sunlight is refracted by the Earth's atmosphere."

"I am *so* not about that red moon right now," Sammy said.

"I dreamed about a red moon and there it is," Neve said.

"It's been in the news for weeks," Piper said. "It might not mean anything."

"It looks like a tomato," Neve said.

"You know," Piper said, and her voice sounded like she was smiling, "it kind of does."

"And there's something else," Sammy said, pointing the light ahead.

A large hedge blocked the road. A hedge of thorns.

Chapter Twenty-One

THE HEDGE BLOCKING the road extended into the forest on both sides; each of its white thorns was the span of Neve's hand.

"This is the way we have to go," Neve said. "I know it."

"*Where pine meets thorn*. That's what the man meant!" Sammy said. "Uh-oh."

"And what the woman meant when she said we weren't getting in," Piper said. "Obviously."

Ever so gently, Neve touched a thorn. A stab of pain. "Okay, ouch."

"Not going through those," Sammy said. "But maybe we can jump over."

"That hedge is like ten feet high," Piper said.

"I'm thinking pole-vault. I'm going to look for a big stick." He went off with the cell phone light.

"You are *not* going to be able to do that." Piper followed him, continuing to argue.

Neve was left with the blood moon as the only light, and something became visible on the air. Shiny silver sparks, tiny ones, coming over the hedge from someplace on the other side.

Magic.

They were in the right place.

Maybe inside the hedge, there'd be a castle, like in the fairy tale about Briar Rose. Or maybe a shabby hut with a hot oven and that woman laughing wickedly, like in Hansel and Gretel.

But how would Neve rescue Rose even if she got inside? It didn't seem likely it was going to be as easy as pushing the woman into an oven. And what if there were *two* women, like Piper thought?

"Ticktock, watch the clock."

Neve flinched. "Who's that? Who's there?"

"You're running out of time." The source of the voice was over her head, a dark blot of shadow midway up a tree. The raspy voice sounded very familiar. The boy in the red shirt. The boy-who-was-not-a-boy.

"I can't see you. Come down from there," Neve said.

"Not until you have killed her and broken the spells."

"Why are you in a tree? Were you following us?"

"If I had not, I would not have known the way."

"Why are you here? *What* are you?" Neve said.

"A rude question. Though I think you know. You found the statue. You read the story."

"The story from the book? It was you who left it?"

"Naturally, it was I who left the book. As it was I who drew the knife. A magical knife for a magical death. Her death is the only way to break the spells. And you must arrive before midnight if you want to save your sister."

181

"How do you know that? And why do you care?"

"She has something of ours. We want it back. And I cannot go in myself. She has kept us away for . . . some time."

Neve considered. "The golden cup."

There was a long moment where the only sound was Sammy and Piper arguing in the distance. And then the boy-who-was-probably-a-dwarf said, "Yes, the cup. But know this: If you try to take the cup for yourself, I must defend it. I will kill you."

"I don't want a cup."

"That is what they all say at first."

"No, I really *don't* want it. It sounds like very bad news. But no matter what, I've got to get inside. How do I get in?"

"I do not know. Only a child can—"

"Fine!" Neve said. "If I have to figure it out by myself, then please leave me alone. I can't concentrate with you hovering around making scary noises."

An indignant huff and then the *scratch-scratch*. The dwarf was departing.

Neve looked back at the hedge.

A memory: Rose wearing tennis clothes. At a match where Neve had been subbed in at number three singles. Rose had said, "Anyone can be beat, Neve. You just have to find the weak spot. There's always one." Neve had hit to her opponent's backhand the entire match and ended up winning in a tiebreak. *Lucky*, she'd thought at the time. But maybe that wasn't all it had been. She'd watched for it, she knew. The weakness. That backhand had been wobbly.

"Anyone can be beat," Neve whispered now. She'd just have to watch carefully for the weakness.

Yes, the hedge was so thick she couldn't see through it. Yes, the thorns covered every inch to the ground, leaving no room for squirming underneath. Yes, it extended clear across the road and off into the woods on both sides. Still . . .

Neve walked along the hedge, stepping into the woods, pine needles crunching under her shoes, as she searched for a break in the shrubs. Maybe a helpful beaver had come along and gnawed a hole in the hedge because it wanted in. Or, more likely, wanted out.

Like Rose, Neve thought. Rose wanted out. Not just out of the place behind this hedge, but out of Etters. *Coach Ellen says now's the time to make plans if I want to get somewhere with tennis.* Rose had said it herself. She was trying to get somewhere. Somewhere without Neve. Maybe Rose was tired of the two of them doing everything together. And maybe Neve was like the thorn hedge holding her in, and Rose was like the desperate beaver trying to get out.

They did not leave each other. They did not.

Or maybe they did.

"No," Neve said aloud.

"Neve!" Piper called from the road. "Where are you?"

"Here!" Neve called back. At that moment, a root tripped her. She threw out her hands to catch herself and ended up hitting a tree.

It seemed to come out of nowhere. A white oak, distinctive

in this forest of pines. Gnarled and ancient, covered in moss, the oak went up, up, and up. And the red moon glowed on a large limb that extended over the hedge. A limb that looked just sturdy enough to hold a smallish girl. One who very much wanted a way across the hedge.

"That's more like it." Neve hastily pulled her hair into a bun. She put her backpack on the ground and took off her shoes. "I'm climbing a tree!"

"I'm right here." Piper was next to her.

"Sorry. I didn't see you there. I'm going to give this a try." The lowest branch was much higher than Neve's head; she couldn't reach it.

"You're really going to climb it?" Piper said.

"Yep." On Neve's first attempt, her feet slipped. She removed her socks and put them in her pocket, then made a running start at the tree.

Her bare feet worked better. And the bark held beneath her fingers. Breathing in that familiar vanilla-and-vinegar bark smell, she scraped her arms but shimmied up ably enough. Her hands and feet just seemed to know where to go. *I'm a good climber*, she thought. She'd forgotten that. When she was small, she'd always been the best of the neighborhood kids at climbing trees.

She swung her leg over the lowest branch, pulled herself up, and looked down at Piper.

Piper made several jumps at the tree, with no luck. And Neve was already too high up to help her.

"This isn't right," Piper said, out of breath. "It needs to be me that goes. I'm the one who's been looking for so long. I'm the one who figured out the clue in the book. I'm the one who knew this was a magic road."

"You can do it. We can all go."

"I doubt it. I can't do the rope climb in gym or a single pull-up. I'm hopeless."

"No, you're not," Neve said.

But Piper was taking off her backpack and digging around inside. A few moments later, she handed up Neve's backpack. "I put something in there. For luck."

Neve felt the weight of it as she put it on her back. "Is it a tomato?"

"I brought it for Jannie. It's from Piper vine. The vine she named after me. I've never grown one like it. It's big and beautiful and perfect. Just like her."

"I'll take the luck, but you're coming too," Neve said.

"I have to know," Piper said. "I have to know what happened to her. We have to find out. I can't live another day if I don't find out."

Neve's heart twisted. She said, with more confidence than she felt, "We will. I know we will. Now go and get Sammy to give you a leg up. You are *not* hopeless. You're more full of hope than anyone I know."

"I'm not hopeless," Piper repeated as she ran to find Sammy. "I can do it."

Neve hugged the trunk as she scrambled higher. She reached the limb she'd been aiming for, and it felt strong. But it was hard to tell if it would hold her. And the tricky part was next—scooting out over a hedge with thorns sharp as needles.

Regardless, she had to do it.

You must arrive before midnight, the dwarf had said. And he'd seemed convinced she was running out of time. She couldn't wait any longer.

"Psst, guys," Neve said. "I'm going over!"

Moving carefully, she slid along the limb, bark crumbling beneath her. *So far, so good. Just a little bit more.* It was only when she was halfway across that it came to her that she didn't have a plan for getting down. She'd have to swing down somehow. And the limb was thinning; she could nearly close her fingers around it.

To make herself lighter, she shrugged off her backpack and tossed it over the hedge. In doing so, she bounced a little.

A creaking sound. The branch shifted slightly downward. *Uh-oh,* she thought, scooching desperately along. Piper and Sammy were shouting from somewhere.

With a loud, final-sounding crack, the branch broke off.

And Neve fell.

Chapter Twenty-Two

MRS. KATCH HAD once been different.

It wasn't Mother who had changed her. Oh, no. Dealing with Mother had been necessary, and it was so long ago that she had practically forgotten. She never thought about Mother at all.

It was the robin.

The red-breasted bird had arrived in the warmth of a spring that was just like every other spring, just as the robin was like every other robin (there had been so many springs and robins that she barely noticed them passing by anymore). But on that particular spring day, that specific robin in the birch tree chirping its blamed head off made her sister say, "Will you look at that little fellow? So happy! I wonder where he's been. I wonder where he'll get off to after this."

Mrs. Katch—though she'd had another name then—had laughed and shrugged and continued her picking of mushrooms and had not wondered about it because back then, she never wondered about robins or places that weren't the swamp.

As it turned out, that was the beginning of everything that happened after, everything that ended with Sister dressing up in that silly hat with the feather and saying she had to go and see the other places for herself before it was too late.

"You can't take it with you," Mrs. Katch said, meaning the golden cup, because she was angry at Sister for leaving and, even more, for not suggesting she go too, even though she didn't want to and she knew Sister knew that. "You'll start to age, and who knows what'll happen then?"

"It's all right," Sister said. "I want you to have it." And her smile wasn't even sad because she was leaving and she was happy to go.

And when Sister returned all those years later, she'd *still* been happy, even though they'd been separated for such a long time and even though it was too late. Much too late. Too late for the golden cup to save her.

It was too late to save Mrs. Katch too. Or, at least, to save the person she had once been.

For when the first robin appeared the spring after Sister left, Mrs. Katch caught the bird with her bare hands and twisted its neck. The surprised expression on its tiny dead face made her laugh.

It was the moment she decided to shed her old name. The name that meant "pathetic" and "someone who cared too much" and "someone who got left behind." The name she forgot almost immediately.

She began to call herself Mrs. Katch.

She was much happier that way.

Chapter Twenty-Three

NEVE LANDED in a pear tree. Or, more accurately, she collided with the branches of a pear tree in a jumble of limbs and hair and leaves.

Then — *thud!* — she was lying on the ground, flat on her back, staring up at a spinning night sky.

Oh no, she thought. *The branch broke. They can't follow me.*

But she wasn't alone. Something was there in the dark. That something descended on her, wet and foul-smelling, and licked her face. She nearly jumped out of her skin before she realized it was . . . the hound! The hound had found her. *Hurry*, he seemed to be saying. *Get up.*

"I'm okay," she said to him.

But the night sky wouldn't stop spinning.

The pear tree came into focus. The large limb that had broken off with her was suspended in the branches directly above her head.

She moved fast then, rolling out from under the limb just before it slid down with a *thump!* And sitting up, still a little dizzy, she found she was in a small orchard, decaying fruit around her.

The hound's cold nose was on her ear, her neck, her arm. Checking on her, she knew.

"Bear. Is that your name?" Neve said. "Do you belong to her?"

His tail wagged in the dark, almost frantically. He nudged her hand. *Yes, it is!* and *Nope, I don't!* she thought he meant.

"Am I just the first person to be nice to you? Is that why you like me?" Neve asked as she scratched behind his ears. She understood that. Who wouldn't want to be around people who were nice? And that woman, it was clear, was anything but. Maybe he'd been hoping to be found by somebody, anybody, else.

Neve took a deep breath, then wished she hadn't. She remembered that pungent smell from being at the gardening store with Mom. *Peat.* It came from somewhere nearby. After getting to her feet, Neve picked squished pears from her jeans.

Her backpack was a few feet away. She felt more secure with it on.

"Sammy," she whispered through the hedge. "Piper!"

They should have been able to hear, but they didn't respond. Someone else did.

"If you are successful," the dwarf said through the hedge, "they will be returned to you."

"What? You did something to them? What did you do to them?"

"Let us just say they await you eagerly," the dwarf said.

Neve pointed at the hedge. "You had better not hurt my friends."

"You had better not fail."

She felt like crying then. But of course, that would have been useless. "I don't know where your rotten cup is. I don't care about your cup. If I see it, I'm going to throw it away." A long pause while Neve glared at the hedge.

"I have done nothing to them," the dwarf finally responded in a peevish tone. "They are here as before, bickering in that absurd manner. You cannot hear their foolishness because the hedge is enchanted. But no doubt they *would* sorely grieve if you fail. Just do your job and all will be restored."

The dwarf wouldn't hurt them, Neve thought. He hadn't hurt Sammy all those years ago, or her, even though he'd had the chance. He just wanted his cup. She hoped.

"I will. You just leave them *alone*." She left the hedge and began to pick her way through the rotten fruit, through the trees, cursing the dwarf for his veiled threats, cursing herself for talking Piper and Sammy into coming, and cursing the absence of her *shoes*. The hound trotted next to her.

Beyond the stand of trees, a house came into view, a large one, on a hill a short distance away, the red moon behind it. It was dark inside; there were no lights to be seen. Except . . . yes, there were faint sparks coming from the house. Magic. Rose must be inside. The woman must be there too. Did she know Neve had made it over the hedge? Surely the woman couldn't have heard the branch breaking. Even if she had, she'd have no way of knowing it was Neve who'd caused it.

Neve stopped short. She had bigger problems than a noisy

arrival. Because between her and the house was . . .

Fog.

It hung over a swamp bed, a bed that stank of peat. And, oh yeah, it was *the* fog. Whispering, just as it had been when Rose was swept away. When the woman was on the road. Invisible eyes turned Neve's way. She felt them.

"You took her," Neve said, heart beating fast.

The whispers grew louder. She could almost make out the words but not quite.

"Right. Just going another way here. Don't mind me." Neve turned on her heel in a deliberate manner and walked along the length of the swamp bed, eyeing the fog as she went; the hound followed her. The fog stayed inside the banks, making no move in her direction. After a short time, though, she came to a row of dense evergreens that completely blocked the path.

"That's no problem. That's fine." She turned and retraced her steps, passing the remains of the orchard, continuing to carefully avoid the fog. As she went, the swamp bed curved with the hedge. It circled the house, she suspected. Like some sort of horrific moat. A big old buffer.

Rose was like that, Neve thought. A buffer between Neve and the world. Between Neve and Dad. Just the other day, in the car with Dad, Rose had made that comment about Neve having the idea for warming up. A simple lie, sure, but Rose did that sort of thing often, had been doing it for as long as Neve could remember, and, Neve recalled now, Rose's voice had actually sounded a little pained.

What an awful spot for Rose to be in, constantly feeling like she had to be Neve's defender. It must have been hard for Rose. Truly, that would have given anyone a headache.

Neve had never thought about that before.

* * *

The hound had been trotting at Neve's heel the whole time.

She stopped. He stopped.

"Do you have any ideas?" she said.

He wagged his tail.

"Doesn't seem like a good idea to walk through it, does it?"

More of the wagging, maybe because she was looking at him and he wanted to be scratched. Or maybe because he *did* think she should walk through it.

"I don't want to," she said. "It might eat me. Plus, I'm barefoot."

His tail paused mid-wag.

"You think I should? Is this a trick?"

He tilted his head to the side. His ears flopped.

"Here we go, then," she said. "Death by cute dog." She put on her socks—which weren't much protection but were better than bare feet—took a deep breath, and stepped closer to the fog.

A buzz of excitement, anticipation, from the mass of gray.

"You," Neve said to the fog, her heart in her throat, "are nasty."

She lifted her foot to take a step forward.

Yip! from the hound.

Neve teetered and put her foot down.

He nosed her hand.

"You want to be scratched right now? Really?" She tried to give him a scratch but he pulled away and yipped again.

So a scratch wasn't what he wanted. What was it, then?

He nosed her hand for the second time. Wagged his tail.

"Oh. You want me to hold on to you," she said.

Since he didn't have a collar, she grabbed his scruff, the thick skin on the back of his neck. He didn't seem to mind.

He stepped down into the swamp bed and she went with him.

Into the fog.

Beyond her outstretched hand on the dog, everything was gray. The smell of peat, of decay, was nearly overwhelming. There wasn't any water in the swamp, but the mucky bottom squished beneath her toes. So much for her socks. Dozens of eyes watched her. She couldn't see them but she could feel them. She heard faint voices too. It was hard to tell what they were saying. They talked over one another. She strained her ears.

Fleeessshhh.

Okay, maybe she didn't need to know what they were saying.

At that moment, she tripped, lost her grip on the hound, and landed on her hands and knees in the mud.

There was a change then. *Shhh,* the voices in the fog said almost happily. She caught a glimpse of what had tripped her. A fox. Just its head. There was also a deer, flattened, its eyes hollowed out. Lots of bones. The fog was closing in around her, covering her like a blanket.

She tried to get up. But the blanket of fog was heavy on her shoulders and her hands seemed to be stuck, the mud hardening around her fingers. Panic seized her. "You can't have me!" she said, her voice swallowed by the fog. After yanking desperately, she finally got one hand out. But the other was still stuck.

A whimper. She couldn't help herself. But actually, the whimper wasn't coming from her. It was the hound, right there, his body warm against her leg. She grabbed him and managed to get her other hand out. The pressure left her shoulders.

Shrieking disappointment, the fog churned around her, tearing at her clothes, her hair.

She kept an even firmer grip on the hound this time. There were more things beneath her, tripping her up. Bigger things. Hard things. Bone-like things. She didn't look down again, just continued to take one step, then another.

It felt like forever. Months. Days. Though it was probably only about five minutes. Her shin hit a shelf of earth. She was across.

She scrambled out, following the hound. She'd made it through. The fog was not coming after her. It stayed in its banks, though it still swirled angrily, grumbling and complaining. She eyed it there. No, none of those bones were Rose's. They *couldn't* be. The woman had said *she* had Rose. And the dwarf had said Neve was running out of time but that Rose could still be saved;

Neve just needed to get there before midnight. And Neve herself felt Rose was in the house. Still, Neve's chin wobbled.

The hound licked her hand.

"How is it that *you* get a pass to cross?" Neve said. How was he leading her? Why was he leading her?

No, she couldn't worry about that. It wasn't as if he would be able to explain it. And he only wanted to help, she felt sure of it.

She took off her socks and left them on the ground; they were caked with mud and reeked of the swamp bed. Barefoot again, she took a step toward the house. *Crunch.*

Beetles, roaches, centipedes. The yard was teeming with bugs. Neve wasn't particularly squeamish about insects, but this was ridiculous. She gritted her teeth and tried to ignore the sounds beneath her toes as she walked to the house. *Crunch. Crunch. Crunch.*

An object was on the ground, reflecting the moonlight. It took Neve a moment to recognize it.

Rose's stainless-steel water bottle. The one she'd carried on her run.

Neve picked up the bottle, shook the insects from it. It was full of dents, as if someone had lobbed it down a mountain multiple times.

She hugged it to her chest. She was in the right place.

Rose.

Chapter Twenty-Four

ROSE WAS STILL bound to the chair. As a pot on the woodstove bubbled and spit, she moved her tongue over the place where her tooth used to be.

"You've got a tooth, blood, hair," Rose said. "You can let me go now." The gap between her teeth made it difficult to chew the dried apple pieces and bits of bread Mrs. Katch had set in front of her, though Rose was getting good at picking up the food with her lips.

Mrs. Katch was pouring salt on the kitchen floor, drawing a large circle with it. "Oh no, little fish, you are not off the hook. There is more to be done."

While the woman's back was turned, Rose hurriedly used her chin to slide the deer-hoof knife off the table and into her lap. She cleared her throat. "What else could you need? Fingernails? A urine sample?"

Mrs. Katch laughed. "I need my dearest companion, that's what I need. And it won't be long now. Once I have the final ingredient for the brew, she will drink it and we will be together again as we are meant to be."

Rose resisted the urge to glance over at the corpse. Mrs. Katch's insistence that she could bring it back to life was disturbing, to say the least. She talked to the corpse often and with affection, assuring it the spell would work this time. And a golden cup waited next to the bubbling pot on the woodstove. But how was the corpse supposed to *drink* from that? It didn't have much of a throat—no, Rose really didn't want to imagine it. With her knees, Rose gently shifted the knife in her lap toward her reaching fingers. The knife must've been sharp. She caught sight of the blood on her bare thigh before she felt the sting of the cut and grimaced as she kept shifting.

"What are *you* doing here?" Mrs. Katch said.

Rose started and nearly knocked the knife from her lap, but the woman wasn't talking to her.

The fog hung in the window, blocking the view, so dense that it was nearly white. Voices came from the fog, words unintelligible.

Rose cringed. She couldn't help it.

"Yes, of course I know that," Mrs. Katch said. "But you'll have to wait until the last stroke of midnight for your meal." And to Rose: "No need to look so alarmed. *You* won't go to the fog. That'll be the other."

"The other?" Rose said. "What other?" A sinking feeling. She already knew.

"Who do you think?" Mrs. Katch said. "A most beloved sister, you are. Worth a lot of trouble, apparently. She's trying to get to you. Though I expect she'll be sorely disappointed. And you have her to thank for your predicament, you know. The spell requires a *beloved* sister. If she disliked you, little fish, I'd never have reeled you in to begin with."

"Neve," Rose whispered.

Chapter Twenty-Five

NEVE WALKED THE bug-infested ground toward the strange house, feeling the occasional sting as an insect bit a bare foot. No light anywhere except for the glow of the red moon and the faint sparks of magic that seemed to be coming from the back of the house.

The hound dashed to a front window, turned, and yipped.

Neve paused. "You think I should go that way? Why? The magic is in the back, isn't it?"

He made a strangled sound. It was obvious he thought this was the way to go. And he'd gotten her through the fog, hadn't he?

"Oh, all right," she said.

The window ledge felt coated in slime. She hoisted herself up. The sash was jammed open and looked as if it'd been that way for some time. Neve swung her leg over the sill and pushed back a curtain, stiff with mold.

The hound watched from below.

"You're not coming?" Neve said, then realized it was too high for him to climb up. She would have to go on by herself. He looked very small down there. "Okay, my dear Bear. Wish me luck," she said.

A damp carpet squelched beneath her toes. Inside was even darker than outside. She felt spiderwebs against her cheeks. Smelled rot and decay, like an animal had come in and died. The air was cold and still. Once she got a few steps in, the carpet was drier.

She walked with her hands out in front of her to make sure she didn't run into anything. But she did run into something. A piece of furniture of some sort. She traced it with her fingertips. Torn cloth, cold buttons. A couch.

A squeak and a scuttling from somewhere. The faint sound of fluttering wings.

She passed through a doorway. Got a sense of the space opening up, the ceiling higher. The air flowed better. A large window let in more moonlight. A crystal chandelier layered with spiderwebs gave off the barest sheen. It was a foyer.

A moving figure gave her a fright until she realized it was her own reflection in a dusty mirror.

A woman's chanting voice came from the back of the house, through a door leaking a flickering light. That must be Neve's destination. She was close now.

But then, a frail, quavery voice: "Care to make a trade, dearie?"

The voice belonged to an old woman in a black dress sitting on a stool by a hearth in a parlor. The crackling fire revealed her wizened face. Odd that Neve hadn't noticed the light before.

"A trade for what?" Neve whispered because this wasn't the woman she was looking for — this one was much too old — and Neve didn't want the woman with the fog to hear. Neve needed to spy on that woman, see what was going on, before deciding what to do.

The old woman eyed her. "That hair. So pretty and longy-long."

Neve put a hand to her hair. It fell over her shoulders like a sheet. "No, I don't think so. I like my hair where it is."

"I'm not asking for *all* of it. Just a snippet now, poppet. And in return, I'll give you knowledge of what you'll encounter in the circle."

"The circle?"

"It's where you're going, is it not?" She nodded toward the back of the house, where the chanting was coming from.

Neve didn't know what the circle was, but she couldn't risk turning down knowledge that might help. "Okay."

As soon as Neve agreed to the bargain, the woman leaped up in a shockingly agile fashion, brandished a set of silver shears, and lopped off a hank of hair at the level of Neve's chin.

"Hey!" Neve protested. It was a lot of hair. The woman hadn't been entirely truthful about that.

"What do you think about me now?" The woman's few teeth shone in the firelight as she cackled, the shining ribbons of Neve's hair displayed on the balding head. "Am I so very beautiful?"

"Um. It's nice like that, I guess. But what about the knowledge you owe me?"

The woman settled back down on her stool, stroking her new hair. "Ah yes, your knowledge. It is this: in the circle, you must face that which you most fear if you are to achieve your aims."

"But I know that already. I'm afraid of that woman. And I've got to defeat her."

The old woman tut-tutted. "Doireann is not your greatest fear. You must look deeper than that, poppet. What is it you *most* fear?"

"Not to be able to save Rose."

The woman shook her head. "Deeper again, dearie. What has been driving you the entire journey? Causing you to do braver things than you ever thought possible? You did those things because they weren't as terrifying as the *worst* thing. The thing you *most* fear."

Neve found she *did* know what it was. She did not say it out loud. She could not. It was selfish, that fear. She was embarrassed by it.

The woman cackled. "I see that you do know it. Very good. Now you will have the strength to do the last brave thing, and that is to kill Doireann. It's no more than she deserves. The murderous wretch! I've been waiting a long time for her to get her comeuppance. The knife—you must get the knife. Slip it right into her heart. You will do what needs to be done and you will save your sister to boot. But you're running out of time. Go!"

A shower of sparks came from the fire, and Neve threw up her hands to protect her face. When she opened her eyes, the old woman was no longer there. The stool, barely visible in the moonlight shining through the windows, was empty. There was no fire in the hearth. How had the woman put out the fire and left so quickly?

The old woman wasn't behind Neve. Or hanging from the ceiling like a spider.

Neve blinked at the fireplace. It was covered in some type of grate. She touched it. Cold. And no lingering smell of burning wood.

It was as if that old woman had never been there at all.

Neve tucked one side of her hair behind her ear. It slipped out against her cheek. Yes, a large section had been chopped off. An icy feeling traveled down her spine.

The mother. The one who had traded her daughter away. The one whom the other daughters had stabbed until she was *dead.*

Neve heard baying from the hound somewhere. She had to hurry.

Trying not to look back, she tiptoed down the hall, the faintest giggle in the air behind her.

* * *

Light bled from under the door. A woman's voice was behind it.

Neve took a deep breath, clearing her mind like she did before a math test. She gently pushed open the door and peered inside.

A kitchen. Flickering light from a woodstove and an assortment of candles.

Bad smells. Very bad.

"Finally!" someone said.

The woman who had been on the road. Rose was there too, in a chair, bound with ropes, still in her running clothes. Both looked as if they'd been expecting Neve. In another chair was a figure that looked like a Halloween display, though Neve had the horrible feeling that it wasn't.

"Cut it a little close, didn't you?" the woman said. "We've only got minutes and I need that final ingredient from you. *Tears of regret*. And you will shed them, as terribly unsuccessful as you're going to be at saving your sister. As hard as I've made you work getting here. You'll shed buckets of them, I'm sure."

Rose said quickly, "She's going to push me in, Neve. She needs to sacrifice a soul but she also needs your tears. Don't cry afterward. Don't give her the satisfaction. Don't let the spell work. And watch out for the fog."

In?

The woman was talking, saying something about how clever she was for having figured out the spell this time, how the translations were so tricky. While she spoke, Neve tried to take in something else.

The large circular hole in the floor between her and Rose, as big as a kitchen table. Though it didn't seem to be *in* the floor, exactly. It didn't reveal a view of the basement. Inside was another world. A sky of purple, with shining streams of silvery air. Dark shadowy shapes flying around.

"Neve," Rose said. "Look at me."

Neve glanced up.

Rose had a knife. *The* knife. A handle that was made of a deer hoof. Rose's wrists were bound, but she held the knife, and she was going to flick her hand, toss the knife to Neve, Neve could tell, over the hole. Neve knew Rose could do it. As many drills as Rose had done tossing that tennis ball, she could do it. And the woman didn't see it there. And Neve knew what Rose wanted. She wanted Neve to kill the woman, just like the dwarf wanted, just like the ghost of the mother wanted.

But Neve saw something else. The woman was right behind the chair, and she was going to shove Rose into the hole, into the other world, chair and all. And Neve might be able to kill the woman, might be able to stab her through the heart as instructed, but Rose would already be gone.

And so, even as the knife arced through the air, Neve did the only thing she could do, the only thing that made sense to her, because after all that had happened, after all she had learned, she wasn't doing what others told her to do. She was doing what *she* would do.

She jumped.

Chapter Twenty-Six

AS SHE FELL, Neve met the woman's eyes. Wide eyes. The woman hadn't expected Neve to jump, that was clear. If nothing else, Neve had managed to surprise her.

The hole closed behind her like a great mouth shutting, and she was in the other world. Because she'd faced it. Her greatest fear.

Being alone. Just plain old Neve. Without Rose.

A lost puzzle piece. A broken scissor. A fallen branch.

Definitely *fallen*. And *falling*. Maybe that's what this place was, endless falling.

Deciding to jump hadn't been hard. Actually, it had been easy. Neve had done it because she didn't want Rose's soul to be the one sacrificed. She hadn't had time to think about it, to dread it, to expect much of anything from this place. But so far, she was . . .

Fine. She hadn't crash-landed. In fact, the falling had slowed and she was floating, drifting along on a silvery stream. The air was comfortably warm and smelled of springtime. Other shapes floated above her, below her. Lumpy, shadowy shapes. None of them looked like anything in particular.

Except for the tomato.

Piper's good-luck tomato. It floated next to her, a wink of orangey red in the purple sky.

"You escaped my backpack, I see. Where are we?" Neve said. She could see through her hands to the sky beyond. Her skin was a shimmery blur. Actually, it was radiant. She *glowed*. "I guess I'm a ghost. Do you think this is air? What *is* this place?"

But the tomato was floating away.

"Wait!" The tomato meant so much to Piper. It seemed important that Neve not lose it. She kicked the air, swam after it through the silver streams. The tomato was going down, though it seemed to sink with purpose, moving faster. She followed it through layers of the airstreams, the purple sky deepening in color.

Finally, the tomato came to a stop, landing atop a shadowy smudge about Neve's size. A smudge that seemed to be floating on its back, hands behind its head.

"Oh, hello," Neve said. "Is this your airstream?"

The shadowy smudge laughed, a tinkling sound. "Not hardly. Is this your tomato?" A girl's voice, Neve thought.

Neve smiled. "No, it's its own tomato. And it wanted to go here to you, I think."

The shadowy someone moved her head—or the round blotch of shadow that seemed to be her head—closer to the tomato. Sniffed. A glimpse of curly hair. "Piper vine. I thought so. I smelled it coming."

"It's still alive, that vine." Neve realized she was repeating something Piper had said. "Piper brought the tomato for . . . well, she brought it for you, I think. Are you Jannie?"

"Piper is here?"

"No. She tried to come. She wanted to come. But the branch broke off, you see."

"And it ended up being you. You were in the house of the cailleach? Of Mrs. Katch?"

"I don't know her name. She was in the fog."

"That's her, all right. Still trying to bring her sister back to life, I expect. She's been trying for years."

"Oh. Her sister . . . I think I saw . . . well, her sister looked pretty dead to me."

"Without a doubt. The spell will not work. It will never work. Her sister has gone on. But Mrs. Katch is nothing if not stubborn."

"Rose said Mrs. Katch needed a soul and that she needed tears. Tears of regret. She was going to push Rose in and use my tears. But I jumped into . . . here . . . instead."

"Ah. I see. A willing sacrifice. 'The best rosebush, after all, is not that which has the fewest thorns, but that which bears the finest roses.'"

"That's pretty. What does it mean?"

"It means life can be hard sometimes, but it's what you do with what you have, what choices you make, that matters. You remind me of that quote. Because you jumped."

"Piper would have jumped too. She misses you. She looks for you all the time."

"I miss her too. Though it's different here. The man who said that about roses also said this:

> Time is
> Too slow for those who wait,
> Too swift for those who fear,
> Too long for those who grieve,
> Too short for those who rejoice,
> But for those who love,
> Time is not.

"That's beautiful," Neve said. "I see what you mean."

Jannie took the tomato in a shadowy hand, floated upright. "So, tears of regret. That's a new one. Do you think she got the tears for her spell?"

"I don't think so. Rose wouldn't have wanted to give them to her."

"No doubt the cailleach couldn't produce any of her own. Not that the tears would help her anyway. A willing sacrifice doesn't count. And I see that you haven't been here long. You can't have been, not with this fruit, not with that glowing aura." Jannie made a loud trilling sound. It wasn't harsh. It was more like a bird's call. "Don't worry, we're going to help you. We've been waiting here for this sort of chance."

Soon, there were a dozen other shadowy someones floating companionably around Neve.

"Hello," Neve said.

A round of hellos. All girls.

While Neve floated there, Jannie and the others spoke to one another with soft, musical words that Neve couldn't understand. Then Jannie whispered something to the tomato and swished it over to the next shadowy someone, who captured the tomato and passed it on. A slow-moving game of toss.

"What are you doing with the tomato?" Neve opened and closed her fingers, letting the iridescent air gleam between them.

"We're giving it our blessing. And we're sending it back with you. You will not share our fate. When you go back, you must find the small green book. And you must destroy it. It is the source of her magic. She won't be able to do this again."

"Back? I can go back?" Neve said. "But the hole closed behind me after I jumped."

"We have hope it will open for you. You found us so quickly. It usually takes ages of floating around before we find each other. And by then the fog has come . . . so, anyway, a bite of tomato is what you'll need. One bite will be enough. Don't forget. Don't forget *us*. We, all of us, are giving you this chance to stop her. You mustn't waste it. Tell Piper the things in Meemaw's mason jar are for her. The jar that was under my bed. I'll be moving on, but tell her I love her. That I always will."

"I'll tell her." The tomato was tossed Neve's way and she caught it. "But can you explain what to do?"

"There's no time. But we believe in you," Jannie said. "You can do this."

And then they were all clustered around Neve, whispering good wishes, shadowy hands together giving her a push. *Up.* And before she quite realized what was happening, she was high above them, powerful wings beating at her back. She could feel the wings, see them. Wide, white wings. She was moving them herself. They were *hers*. And she glowed, bright and strong, as she went up and up and up, faster and faster, until she was . . .

Out.

Chapter Twenty-Seven

A CLOCK WAS chiming the hour. Midnight.

Neve was in Mrs. Katch's kitchen. The wings were gone. The hole in the floor was gone. She was solid again.

Rose's chair was overturned in the spot where the hole used to be, Rose still attached to the chair. She'd managed to free a hand and was struggling with Mrs. Katch, who was on the floor and had her by the ankle.

"You have to stay!" Mrs. Katch yelled. "Give me my tears!"

Rose had knocked over her own chair, Neve suspected. Rose had been trying to go too. To go with Neve into the purple sky.

In their struggle, they must've knocked into the corpse.

The fancy hat with the feather had fallen off, along with a headful of gray hair. A patchy and torn sheen of skin—the skull showing through. Pearl earrings sagged from the remains of the ears.

The corpse was just as dead as before.

Neve was standing next to a small green book, she realized. The book was on the kitchen counter, just lying there. Surely it was the right one. There were no other books in sight. Neve held the tomato carefully in one hand; she snatched the book with the other.

Mrs. Katch looked up. And, oh yeah, she had not expected to see Neve. All traces of that mocking smile were gone.

Surprise! Neve wanted to say. But she was too surprised herself. The book did not feel like she'd expected. It was heavier than it should have been for its size, and the cover was rough and bumpy, like the skin of a reptile. Even worse, the book whispered to her. An unfamiliar word, but it sounded like the same word that wrote *itself* on the book's cover in black ink, over and over. *Seunachd.*

It was repulsive. The last thing Neve wanted to do was hold that book. But the girls were depending on her.

A bite of tomato. Jannie had said that. Neve bit into the tomato like an apple. She felt better at once.

The final stroke of midnight.

Then, from behind her, words spoken by many voices talking together: *The spell is finished. What is left is for us.* It was the fog, creeping in through the door, through the window.

"It makes no difference," Mrs. Katch said, getting to her feet. "Go ahead and clean up this mess. I can't bear to look at it any longer."

By *mess*, she meant them, Neve suspected. Her and Rose. Neve understood what the fog wanted. The fog's specialty was cleaning up. Getting rid of the leftovers. All that endless hunger. Panic shot through Neve's chest.

The fog didn't wrap itself around her, though. Rather, the voices whispered, *Blessed,* and the fog broke around her like a stream breaking around a rock. It swept across the floor toward Rose.

Rose was still trapped in the chair. "Go away!" she cried.

In Neve's hand, the tomato shone brightly. Her good-luck tomato. Her *blessed* tomato.

"Catch!" Neve tossed the tomato to Rose. "Take a bite!"

Rose gave her a puzzled look but she caught the tomato one-handed and didn't hesitate to bite into it.

The fog edged back from Rose.

"What's going on here?" Mrs. Katch said. "Why is everyone eating tomatoes?"

"It's a vegetable that's really a fruit," Neve said. The words just popped out. Piper would have been proud.

The fog moved toward Mrs. Katch.

"Don't expect anything from *me,*" she said to it. "I suppose you're out of luck this time, bottom-feeder."

"Give it to her," Neve said. "Rose, give her the tomato."

"I do *not* consume partially eaten vegetables," Mrs. Katch said.

"But I have the book," Neve said. The source of her magic. "Maybe that means the fog doesn't listen to you anymore."

Mrs. Katch looked uncertain for the first time. "Give that back! You've no right to it. It belongs to me."

Neve took a step away, clutching the book. Though she didn't want it, she couldn't risk giving it back.

The fog moved closer to Mrs. Katch, swirling in an excited sort of way. *You are master of the book no longer.*

"I most certainly am the master. I'm just momentarily missing my book," Mrs. Katch said.

The fog started wrapping around her legs.

"Stop that!" Mrs. Katch said. "I have not commanded you to do that."

"Take a bite of the tomato," Neve said. "It's a blessed tomato!"

Rose tossed it Mrs. Katch's way but she didn't reach for it. The tomato fell to the floor with a small, desolate *splat.*

As Mrs. Katch struggled against the fog, she reached toward the corpse and cried, "Etain!"

Neve couldn't look. It was too much like before, too much like what had happened to Rose. Behind her fingers, she heard Mrs. Katch screaming, screaming.

And then the screaming stopped. A slamming of doors. Silence.

Mrs. Katch and the fog were gone. The corpse was gone too.

✳ ✳ ✳

Several long moments passed before they could speak.

"Well, that was awful," Rose said. Her eyes were red. "Can you hand me that?" She meant the knife on the floor, the one she'd tried to toss to Neve.

Neve handed her the knife, cleared her throat. "About the most awful thing I can think of."

"Maybe not the *most* awful. Thanks to you." Rose managed a small smile before she started cutting the remaining ropes that bound her. "Is that book talking to you?"

Words ran over the cover in black ink, faster now. Words like *Ceò-draoidh, Or-bhàis,* and *Draodhachd.* The book whispered the words to Neve, its tone cajoling, as if it were trying to convince her of something. Though Neve didn't understand the meaning of the words, she felt the power behind them, a cleverness that was almost *alive.* And the horror she'd felt on first holding the book was stronger. It was a wicked thing, that book.

Don't forget us.

Neve owed it to Jannie, to the others, to make sure the book was never opened again.

Beside her, Rose stood unsteadily, free of the ropes. "I think I sprained my ankle." She looked thin. She'd lost weight. For the first time in Neve's life, it occurred to her that Rose was just a girl, not much older than Neve herself. Rose glanced at the book. "What are you going to do with that?"

Once, Neve would have said, *What do you think I should do?* But that wasn't what she said now. "Hand me that knife."

Rose handed it over without question.

The knife with the deer-hoof handle. Definitely the one the dwarf had wanted Neve to stab Mrs. Katch with. But Neve felt a rightness. The knife was more than ready for *this* task.

Neve put the book on the counter, lifted the knife, and brought it down as hard as she could. When the knife pierced the cover, a tingle shot up her arm, so sharp she gasped.

A cry from the book. A shaft of light where the knife had pierced it. The light filled the room for a brief moment, turning Rose's stunned face the palest white, before burning out with a loud popping noise.

A shadow seeped from the book. A shadow that pooled on the counter, gathered itself, then rose to form a figure that grew so tall it touched the ceiling.

It was too late to run.

But the shadow wasn't coming for them. It leaped down from the counter and bled through the floorboards, disappearing from view.

A rumbling beneath their feet. The logs in the woodstove crackled as they shifted. Candles and chairs tumbled over.

Neve let out a breath. "Time to go."

She left the knife in the book and took Rose's hand. They ran out into the night and found that the moon was no longer red. It had turned silver, and the silver light shone on gnarled trees, tall grass, and a dry swamp moat. The fog was gone.

The rumbling still came from the house. A section of the roof collapsed.

They heard people shouting their names. It was Sammy and Piper, being led, at a run, by Bear.

"The hedge just shriveled up," Sammy said. "The dog showed us a bridge."

"You found her!" Piper said. "Did you find anyone else? Anyone?"

"Piper." Neve reached out to take the other girl's hand. "I'm so sorry. There's no one else."

"No one? No, that can't be right," Piper said. "I was going to find her. I was."

"Listen to me," Neve said. "I know this sounds impossible, but Piper, we did find her. Jannie's in a place that seemed like—well, it seemed like heaven. I *saw* her there. I talked to her. She's surrounded by friends. I'll tell you all about it when we're away from here. But she told me to tell you that she loves you. And you know what else? It was your tomato that led me to her. Really, it was your tomato that saved us all."

Piper stared at Neve. She blinked a lot. "She told you she loves me?"

A loud cracking sound. House timbers breaking. A fissure opened up in the ground; two feet wide, it ran just behind them, from the house to the swamp.

"Let's go!" Sammy pulled Piper away. Neve supported Rose as they scrambled to follow, the hound leading them.

"Neve," Rose said. "I have to tell you . . . I need to tell you . . ." She seemed to run out of breath.

"I know about the academy," Neve said. "Don't worry. We can talk about it when we're away from here."

Chapter Twenty-Eight

THEY PAUSED TO look back.

Sammy had a bottle of water he gave to Rose, and she drank from it gratefully.

"Shouldn't we get farther away?" Piper said.

They were back on the road, past the remains of the hedge. The swamp bed seemed unaffected, but Mrs. Katch's house was crumbling into a great hole. The silver light of the moon captured an impressive plume of dust in the air.

"Look!" Sammy said.

Out of the hole, out of the dust, burst the dwarf. He scurried toward them, scrambling through the collapsing earth and then over the stone bridge they'd just traveled.

This time there was no mistaking him for anything *but* a magical dwarf. The boy-disguise was long gone and what remained was a shriveled-up creature with a tall green cap and long white beard who looked to be hundreds of years old. Neve wouldn't have recognized him except for the red shirt and the black boots. A small sack was slung over his shoulder.

"Who's *that?*" Rose said.

"He's been trying to get something from there for a while," Sammy said.

Then the dwarf was past them, faster than Neve would have thought possible, giggling madly. A glimpse of tall slender ears, a mouthful of pointed teeth, eyes like black marbles.

"You owe me a coin!" Sammy shouted after him.

"Check your pack, foolish boy!" the dwarf shouted back.

Sammy swung the pack from his shoulders and dug around inside. "What do you know." He flipped up a coin. It flickered in the moonlight and he caught it. "How'd he do that?"

"I think you know the answer to that," Piper said, but she didn't sound as mean as before. "Plus, you *did* take off your pack while you were doing your pole-vaulting."

"Ha," Sammy said. "If I'd had a decent stick, I'd have made it. I've got a career in that, I think."

Piper said to Neve, "I need to know all of it. I need to know what you saw."

"I'll tell you all the details when we get back to my house. I want to take my time and get it right," Neve said. "But . . . Jannie did tell me that the things in Meemaw's jar, the jar that was under her bed . . . those are for you."

"Meemaw's jar?" Piper breathed. "Oh."

"Why'd the house fall down?" Sammy said.

"I think the magic just ran out," Neve said. "Her spells are broken."

"And where'd that dog come from anyway?" Sammy said.

"He's mine," Neve said. She would not give up until Mom agreed to that.

Sammy's phone sounded. "Cell service is back! I'm calling my mom."

"I've got bars too." Piper started frantically typing on her phone.

"The road is different," Neve said.

And it was. An owl hooted from somewhere. The stars shone through the trees, which rustled softly in a light breeze.

A regular country road at nighttime.

Neve realized something. "Oh! Since the spells are broken, everything will be back to normal. Mom and Dad will be back to normal too." At least she hoped they would be.

"Something was wrong with Mom and Dad?" Rose said.

"I've got a lot to tell you," Neve said.

"Same here. And I feel so bad about Mom. I was acting like such a brat. It all seems so unimportant now. But how'd you find me? How'd you *do* all this? Tell me *some* of it, at least." Rose took another sip from Sammy's bottle of water and leaned on Neve as they walked.

Neve filled Rose in on the main points while they picked their way along the road; neither of them had shoes. The hound trotted beside them, and Sammy and Piper walked ahead, talking on their cell phones.

"You were *all* in on this? Wow," Rose said after Neve finished.

"Yep," Neve said.

"I knew you'd come. I was sitting in this box for such a long time, and after that in that chair, and then, all at once, I remember thinking, *She's on her way.*"

"You were in a box?" A memory of the vision in the fog.

"Yeah, I was. And I did a lot of thinking in there. I want to apologize."

"Apologize? For what?"

"For not seeing how much you do for me. For not noticing how strong you are. I just felt like I knew it all. Telling you to do this and that. I'm sorry. I didn't realize I was being so bossy."

"You didn't make me do things. I *wanted* to do them. Mom told me to do my own thing too, but I wouldn't listen. I just always thought you knew best."

"Why would you think that? How'd that idea even get started?"

Because I thought I was only one-half of a whole. Because I wanted to make sure you loved me. Because I thought, in some secret place inside, that if I acted like you thought I should, Dad might love me too . . . "I was trying to be something I'm not. It was a mistake."

"I don't know about mistakes. But I do know that you're amazing just the way you are."

"My mom's on her way to your house!" Sammy called to them.

Neve gave him a thumbs-up he probably couldn't see. "Listen . . . if you want to go to that academy, I'll be okay. I don't want to go. But I'd be fine in school by myself. I really would."

"Isn't that the truth," Rose said. "You're a superstar. You saved my *life,* Neve. You went to . . . somewhere not here . . . and you *made it back*. You can do anything. And I don't know why I didn't tell you I was considering the academy. I don't know why I was being so secretive about it."

"I know why. Because you were worried about me. Because you thought I might try to follow you to the academy even though I didn't want to go or that I would be a disaster at school by myself. I think you *were* trying to tell me, really. But you don't need to worry about me anymore."

"Yeah. That's pretty clear," Rose said.

"I also need to tell you something. I just need to get it out."

Yes, the pain of the secret was still there. Neve felt it between her ribs, settled in deep. It made her feel both hot and cold. But she *did* need to get it out. Quickly, before she could change her mind, Neve said, "Mom and Dad separated because of me. Because of how he acts toward me. I heard them talking the weekend Mom packed up, so don't tell me it isn't true. That's why we're out here to begin with. It's all my fault." She took a breath, put a hand to her chest.

Rose was quiet for a moment. "Why didn't you tell me you heard that?"

Neve shrugged. She didn't trust herself to speak. She did feel better, having the secret out of her chest. In fact, she would have liked to leave the secret lying right there on the road.

"You know it's not *actually* your fault, right?" Rose said. "Adults do weird and unfair things all the time but *we* can't control what they do. Mom might not even be right about how he feels. She can't see inside his head."

Neve wanted to believe that. She really did.

Rose continued. "And Dad's kind of an — well, you wouldn't want to be married to someone like him, would you? He's kind of . . . overly opinionated, don't you think? He gets on these tangents and just goes *off* on things."

Neve gave Rose a sideways glance. People going off on things sounded awfully familiar. "I guess."

"Mom could just be using you as an excuse. People don't always say what they really mean. Anyway, my point is that it's not on you. It's not on us."

"It still feels . . . hey, I'm not telling you this to make you feel guilty. I don't blame you for how he feels, and I don't think you should blame yourself either."

"I never! I don't ever! Well, maybe I do sometimes. Feel guilty." Rose touched her head to Neve's. They still walked arm in arm, supporting each other. "Though I don't think it's really about me. I think it's more about him. How he always wanted to be this big athlete."

"Try not to feel guilty. It just makes you more stressed."

"I see that. I'll try. No more secrets between us, okay?" Rose said. "Promise me."

"I promise. Pinkie swear." They linked pinkies, then the hound nudged Neve's hand and she stroked his head.

A big barn owl lit out over the road ahead of them, wide wings flapping in the night.

And then flashlights. Shouts. People coming down the road toward them.

"Pops! Bubba!" Piper said, bursting into tears as she broke into a run.

More people. Sammy was hugging an older woman, his mom.

And there were Mom and Dad, running their way, shouting their names.

"How are we going to explain all this?" Rose said. "They're not going to believe it."

"It's a story, all right," Neve said. "We'll tell it together."

Chapter Twenty-Nine

THEY KEPT IT in the spare room of Neve's house.

And then, on a Saturday evening in February, four months after all that had happened with Mrs. Katch and the fog, Neve and Sammy rounded up everyone from the firepit Mom had built in the backyard and crowded them into the small family room.

Rose and her friend Jody sat on the divan, both wearing Etters Academy T-shirts. It turned out Sammy's mom *did* know everyone, and she'd found a retired tennis coach to work with them in the afternoons in nearby Cassatt. The coach even had a court in her backyard. Neve had decided to cut back on tennis, so it was just Rose and Jody so far. Etters Academy was sort of an inside joke. Rose hadn't yet decided about the actual tennis academy for the upcoming school year and no one was pressing her.

Piper, wearing the turquoise-bead necklace Jannie had wanted her to have, was setting vegan caramel apples on a side table. Lately, she and Pops had been getting into apple recipes. The apples were safe on the table; Bear must've learned his lesson about swiping food. After a glance at Neve's mom (who was giving him a stern eye), he did no more than sniff. Since he'd proved to be calm and friendly to everyone, the owner of Prince Gardening Center in Cassatt, where Mom now worked, let Mom take him with her to be an Official Prince Greeter, or so it said on the dapper gold vest they'd gotten him.

Dad was there too, having lately been on his *best behavior* (according to him) and *amicably co-parenting*, which involved, among other things, paying for Rose's private coaching and agreeing to family counseling. Mom and Dad were still separated and that didn't look to be changing, but he *had* been more mellow, Neve decided, at times wearing a mild expression that, he told Neve when she asked about it, meant he was *feeling grateful*. He stood against the wall with Pops, Bubba, and Sammy's mom.

"Check this out!" Sammy said. He held one side of the box's reinforced cardboard base, and Neve held the other. The display, at three feet square, was heavy and hard to carry. They'd built it in the spare room and it was the first time they'd taken it out or shown it to anyone.

"Ta-da," Neve said, feeling her face flush as they set it down. She tucked her hair behind her ears. A shoulder-length bob. She'd had to cut it after the ghost encounter. But she liked the new length. She'd stopped wearing makeup too, except for a strawberry lip gloss Piper had given her. "Mutualistic City," Neve said.

"Wow," Mom said. "That's amazing." Everyone admired it.

The display *was* amazing. Small buildings cut out of cardboard with an X-Acto knife and painted soft colors. Windmills, solar panels, an art fair, a city garden, a hospital, a sports center, a trolley system pulled by little ropes. They'd designed the city together and planned to enter it in the science fair. Mrs. Michaels had also promised extra credit.

"This is a better design for humans to live together and with animals too," Sammy said. "We've got bee habitats, plants for butterflies . . ."

"Nesting places for birds," Neve said, pointing to a garden on top of a building; most of the buildings had them. "Bat houses too."

"The buildings are covered in grass?" Dad said. "Guess that'd make it easier to cool them."

"Like hobbit houses?" Bubba said.

Neve smiled at him. She, Piper, and Bubba had recently finished a Lord of the Rings marathon. "Taller, but that's the idea. Lots of green spaces, even on rooftops."

"I like the trees," Sammy's mom said. "Good placement for shade."

"Where's the pole-vaulting?" Piper said.

"Here!" Sammy said, pointing to a field. There were even miniature shot puts and javelins.

"There's me on the winners' podium," Rose said.

Neve had put tiny figures on a podium next to the track (not the tennis courts). "There're no names on those people," she said with a smile.

"Ah, but I know it's me," Rose said. "And there's the performing arts center named after me." The sign just said PERFORMING ARTS CENTER.

Neve laughed. "Look, Mom." She pointed to something in the city garden.

Mom leaned in closer. "Oh, Neve. Rosebushes. I love them." One red, one white.

There were actually a variety of plants in the garden. Sammy had brought over a huge packet of green tissue paper and they'd gotten a little carried away. Trees, flowers, vegetables of all sorts. But the garden was large and the green spaces were all over.

There was lots of room for growing things.

Acknowledgments

It takes a great deal of effort by a great number of people to bring a book—particularly a debut book!—to readers. Many thank-yous are due. No doubt I'm missing some, but I am indebted to the following:

The entire team at Clarion, especially my brilliant editor, Amy Cloud, for her enthusiasm for this story, along with her spot-on editorial guidance.

My superstar agent, Josh Adams, for his belief in my writing and for being a champion for this book.

The Hamline MFAC program under the leadership of the indomitable Mary Rockcastle and its incredibly supportive community. My accomplished faculty advisors: Jacqueline Briggs Martin, Laura Ruby, Laurel Snyder, and that awe-inspiring force of nature Anne Ursu, who pressed me to finish this story. My fabulous workshop leaders: Elana K. Arnold, Swati Avasthi, Kelly Barnhill, Lisa Jahn-Clough, Nina LaCour, and Claire Rudolph Murphy. And my dearest Mountaineers cohort: Claire Forrest, Megan Matheney, Amanda Moon, and Tracey Sherman, as well as honorary members Anne Cunningham and Nicole Mueller.

Special thanks to Amanda and Austin Moon for their reviews of this manuscript.

My longtime Greenville critique group, mostly scattered now, though together in spirit: Carol Baldwin, Jo Hackl, Sheri Levy, Marcia Pugh, and the late Caroline Eschenberg. Many thanks to Jo for her edits of this book in particular.

Authors Deborah Halverson, Mark Johnston, and Pam Zollman for their invaluable editorial feedback in my early years of writing—yes, I do see now that it can take a long time!

The Branans, Clines, Nelsons, and Antonellis, including my sisters Kinla, Bralie, and Sethley, who inspired this sisterly story and provided much-needed feedback on the manuscript, and my brother, Josh, for his support. My parents, especially my phenomenal mom, who read every page of the FIVE books I wrote before this published one and who encouraged me to keep going.

The Jennings, including my in-laws, Joe and Ann, for their support. My wonderful husband, John, for his loving encouragement. My amazing son Thomas, who patiently read my early books and was always ready with a reassuring word. My equally amazing son Will, who has incredible insight into matters of theme and character.

Thank you. Thank you. Thank you.